When It Burned
to the Ground

When It Burned
to the Ground

Yolanda Barnes

Sarabande Books
LOUISVILLE, KENTUCKY

Copyright © 2005 by Yolanda Barnes

FIRST EDITION

No part of this book may be reproduced without written
permission of the publisher. Please direct inquiries to:
  Managing Editor
  Sarabande Books, Inc.
  2234 Dundee Road, Suite 200
  Louisville, KY 40205

Library of Congress Cataloging-in-Publication Data
Barnes, Yolanda.
    When it burned to the ground / by Yolanda Barnes.— 1st ed.
        p.   cm.
    ISBN 1-932511-18-0 (pbk. : alk. paper)
    1. African American women—Fiction. 2. Los Angeles (Calif.)—
Fiction. 3. Domestic fiction. lcsh I. Title.
    PS3602.A77566W48 2005
    813'.6—dc22   2004023494

13-digit ISBN: 978-1-932-51118-5

Manufactured in Canada
This book is printed on acid-free paper.

Sarabande Books is a nonprofit literary organization.

This project is supported in part by an award from the
National Endowment for the Arts. Funding has also been
provided by The Kentucky Arts Council, a state agency in
the Education, Arts and Humanities Cabinet, with support
from the National Endowment for the Arts.

NATIONAL
ENDOWMENT
FOR THE ARTS

To J.B.B.

In premonition; in odd, disturbing vision: the storefront church bursts with the music of tambourines and tongues of flame.

Before
It Burned to the Ground

The Calling of Daniel

I

Meanwhile, Daniel's calling came. It came during the bright and calcified heat of Indian summer. Although there are no true winters here, not with the severity and hardship of other places. Here winter is the slightest matter of degree, a prissy change in temperament. In exception, of course, there are the torrential rains of February.

His calling could have come during those violent downpours. It could have, but it did not. It came during a heat wave in October as Daniel, dressed in his undershirt and drawers, lay atop his bed. The hour was an opaque one, the atmosphere of the room a prickly dimness gradually shifting into morning; the air was being circulated by a fan. So sweat did not bead on Daniel's forehead until he heard himself being called.

"Daniel," he heard, and he trembled.

"Daniel. I am calling you. Do you hear Me?"

"Yes."

"It won't be an easy life."

"I know," murmured Daniel, frightened for himself.

Finally, Daniel got up and washed his face in the sink. In the closet was a suit; thankfully, it was already pressed. In the drawer of the nightstand was an almost forgotten Bible. It nearly fit in his large palm.

He took a while to polish his shoes. By the time he finished this task, the noise of the birds had been replaced with that of traffic.

Daniel laced his shoes and put on his jacket. All this effort was exhausting. So he sat down in the upholstered chair. The fan had been cut off, and the air in the room was now dense and clogging. His head leaning against the chair's cushioned back, Daniel's breaths were draughts to be swallowed thirstily. With each gulp his Adam's apple bobbed. And he tried to figure a way out.

All the while, softly and diligently, termites were gnawing at the beams and rats were constructing nests in the walls.

And dreading the instinct that guided him, Daniel opened the Bible to find the page that read:

> Then I lifted up mine eyes, and looked, and behold a certain man clothed in linen, whose loins were girded with fine gold of Uphaz:
>
> His body also *was* like the beryl, and his face as the appearance of lightning, and his eyes as lamps of fire, and his arms and his feet like in colour to polished brass, and the voice of his words like the voice of a multitude.
>
> And I Daniel alone saw the vision: for the men that were with me saw not the vision; but a great

quaking fell upon them, so that they fled to hide themselves.

Therefore I was left alone, and saw this great vision, and there remained no strength in me….Yet heard I the voice of his words….

And he said unto me, O Daniel, a man greatly beloved, understand the words that I speak unto thee, and stand upright: for unto thee am I now sent. And when he had spoken this word unto me, I stood trembling. Then said he unto me.

Now I am come to make thee understand what shall befall thy people.

Daniel had read enough. He closed the Book and let his eyes drift shut.

On the nightstand was a phone. It began to ring and ring. Daniel did not raise himself to answer it. When at last it did stop ringing, the din continued in his mind as a distant animal howl which eventually faded into a welcomed period of calm.

That's when he heard his name being called again. "Daniel." This time he heard the impatience.

It takes too much will to struggle against what one has been called to do. So Daniel made himself get up, the unfamiliar weight of the Bible in his unsteady hands.

He owned a brass lamp and a record player and a trunk. He had a framed picture of a mountain peak. Even these few possessions Daniel would have to forfeit. For he had been called now to his new life.

Daniel had two dreams to prepare him for this day.

❖

In the first dream, he stood before a gathering of people. He spoke in tongues. He spoke in a language he did not understand. He spoke with words that had no contours, no boundaries, no letters. His words were actually the notes of a musical composition, a hymn. But it was a mournful hymn and Daniel began to cry. As he cried and sang the sky rained tremendously, flooding the gutters of the dream.

Once Daniel ended the songs and tears, the rain stopped, the sidewalk dried, and instead there was a drought.

❖

In Daniel's second dream he balanced on an anthill. Ants traveled the tawny slopes, crawled into the cuff of his pants leg, journeyed across his starched collar up the incline of his neck. Brother ants. Sister ants. He tried to speak to them, to save their little ant souls.

"I was called," Daniel shouted, but they scurried along. "I was called to tell you something."

❖

So Daniel is to be one of those shouting, arm-waving, dance-stepping men. He is to be part of that legion. So he is to read verse and chapter, recite the poetry of the psalms, call out "Praise Lord" and "Halleluiah." He is to speak of glory and kingdom come, in hollering rants and crescendoing revelation.

And wipe his perspiring face with an already damp handkerchief as he walks a thousand miles in the same pair of shoes, wearing down the heels unevenly, burning holes into the bottoms of the soles.

The intersection corners, the bus stops, the steps of the Water & Power building; these will be his pulpits.

❖

❖

And here was the street that was chosen for him, Piedmont Street. At one time it was prosperous, bright; that was a long while ago. Now it is a dingy cityscape, littered, roamed by stray dogs.

❖

❖

Now Daniel began walking along the avenue that was two flat-roofed rows of petty businesses, of nail salons and we-buy-gold shops, of 99-cent stores and barbeque shacks, of storefront churches and motels.

Among the living exist the dead: buildings that were abandoned, inert; tombs fused with wrought-iron bars, sealed with corrugated doors.

❖

❖

Of course it concerned Daniel that he was being called to a dying breed. When he was a boy it was a different time. Downtown corners northsoutheastwest were the squatter's rights of hoarse-throated, inspired preaching men. Some called during humid, hot weather; some during storms. Some solitary and despised; some leaving behind the domesticity of wives and children. (Oh, He shows no mercy when He calls!)

❖

Daniel, in fact, was a sizeable man, intimidating and glaring. He was often of dangerous moods; he was an arguer and not incapable of threat and tantrum and a pummeling with his fists because most often he found these tactics to be persuasive, even reasonable considering their effectiveness. So for this sort of man to ask with such meekness, with such timidity, "How about I stop and rest a bit?" He was desperate to know, "Would that be all right?"

Came the response only his ears heard, "No. You must keep going, Daniel. You keep going."

❖

A long while and half the length of Piedmont Street he was made to walk. The heel of Daniel's right foot began to chafe. On his left foot a blister tore and bled, soaking the toe of his sock.

❖

Yet it was not until he reached the landmark of the old theater that Daniel finally stopped walking. Upon his arrival here he stood beneath the battered marquee, letters dropped like missing teeth from the last title posted there. He stood in the outer lobby near the ticket box, its window boarded. He rose sequoialike from the rotting green tiles. Black as black can be and a giant, wearing a suit in ninety-degree weather, the Bible in his wet-palmed hands.

Now he was prepared to begin, already sweating

and with a feeling of exhilaration doomed as dawn's blush to be short-lived.

II

From the beginning, Daniel was amazed that the tiredness in him did not reflect in his voice, which was strong and carried far along the street. He did not ramble or hesitate or improvise. He knew exactly what he had to say. And he started with the reminder that this was not their authentic home, that their birthright was a much holier and sacred land, without worry or labor, which now they had become accustomed to. Only man's weakness, he said, led to this exile.

So to call Piedmont Street home is mistaken.

Listen to me.
(I been called to tell ya!)

This is not your home.

It is merely a place where you can give
in to your vices and faults and temptations.
A place where you can
be petty and lustful with each other.

It is a place where you are free to sin
and live in sinfulness.

As you are sinners.

I been called to tell ya.

You are sinners. Let there be no doubt.

You are sinners.

That man leaning a shoulder against the brick wall.
He is a sinner.

That woman sauntering along with no destination.
She is a sinner.

All about are sinners.
Sinners who do their deeds in the boldness of day.

And sinners who every Sunday open their mouths
in praising song to Him,
hoping their chaste clothing, their choir robes and their
holy vestments, will hide their sinful hearts.

Oh!

You who rather gamble away your money than buy
food for your children's bellies.
You who allow connivers and tricksters to take
nourishment at your table,
murderers to sleep in your bed.

Yes, you all are sinners.
And Piedmont Street is seeped in your sins.
This I was called to tell you.

That I am not here today to ask you to repent.

No.
Though you admire your sins more than goodness
and virtue, I do not ask you to repent. You cause
your Lord great sorrow, yet I do not ask you to
repent. I come to you with indictment,

still I do not ask you to repent.
Instead I want to let you know just what your
sinfulness has brought to you.

Are you listening to me?

Because He called me to let you know.

"May your city be cursed," Moses said, "if you do not
hearken the voice of God."

And cursed this place is, Neighbors!

Indeed you are cursed! You are cursed, that's why your
enemies defeat you. You are cursed, beset with tumors,
tormented with dementia. You are cursed with poverty
and crippling, cursed with blindness — AS YOU
REFUSE TO SEE. You are cursed, frustrated in all you
undertake.

Troubles have been brought unto you
and the worse is coming.
Tell 'em, He said. So I'm telling ya.

Oh, yes! It's coming!
It's on its way!

Yes. Yes. Real danger is coming to this place.

Because you have come to the attention of the
devil, my Friends, who is not in repose,
who is not slumbering.
No! He is alive! He is busy!

(Here Daniel thought he heard someone say preach it
so he answered, Yes, I will preach it.)

I've come with a message, Sinners. I've come to let
you know. He called me to tell ya.

That all this time Satan has been festering.
Never has he been at peace.
(I'm telling you, I'm telling. The devil is not at peace.)

What bothers the devil so? Common sense
would think he'd be content, slumped on his
throne, the ruler of his own kingdom where
his vileness reigns absolute.

Yet a sorry kingdom his is.

I come to tell ya.

For company he is surrounded with the de-
spaired, the unsatisfied, the regretful (but too
late, too late they regret). And their society he
despises. At the same time *(I must tell you!)*, he
wants to increase their population, to bring
more of us to this misery. As since he refuses
to allow grace to touch him, he does not
want anyone else to be transformed by its
magnificence.

Listen to me!

In you the devil sees his opportunity.

Yes, the devil sees his chance.

Oh! Listen to me.

He covets Piedmont Street.

I come to tell you.
Listen. Listen.

The devil wants Piedmont Street.

(Now Daniel paused. His own heartbeat swelled, bulged in his ears. He felt the sun and he felt sick. But it was not finished yet so he went on.)

My Brothers and Sisters. I was called. *He* called me. One dazzling morning *He* called me. I schemed and dallied, but *He* kept calling.

"Daniel," He said. It was His voice and I was called.

"Daniel." He called me.

It was not a shout and yet I heard.

So here I am.

You must listen. Listen!

Yes. Here I stand. For the righteous He spares.

(As He saved Noah, a preacher of righteousness, from the flood; as He delivered Lot — that one righteous man dwelling among the sinful, his righteous soul vexed by their unlawful deeds — while turning the cities of SODOM and GOMORRAH into ashes!)

The apostle Peter says, "The Lord knoweth
how to deliver the godly
out of temptation."

So He sent me.
He called me. (So listen to me.)
He wants me to warn you.
He sent me to warn you.

Though it may be preferable not to be among His
anointed. Though it is hard, hard to deliver to you
what I must.

*THE DEVIL'S ALERT, GLEEFUL EYE SEES
THAT YOU HAVE TURNED YOUR BACKS
ON YOUR GOD.*

Yes, the devil knows this. And the devil has a plan.
I've been called to tell you what the devil means to do.
I've come to tell ya. *(I've come to bring-ga ya noos-sa!)*

Satan intends to have proprietorship over
Piedmont Street.

He means to expand Hell's boundaries.

Yes, the devil wants to claim this place.

29

He is on his way!

Listen.

Right now he is on the march, the march, the march.

He has much ground to cover, but he moves swiftly.

Oh, the devil goosesteps this way.

His face is set in smugness for victory he presumes.

Listen to me. Oh, for your own sakes,
you must listen.

My Friends and Neighbors!

What will you do when Satan's army arrives
carrying torches?

Will you welcome the devil?

Will you allow Hell to triumph on Piedmont Street?

Building after building to turn into smokestack,
into chimney, and ruin to prevail?

That is what we are destined to.

Yes, that is our fate.

Our doom.

                              The day is coming,
                                my dear Friends,
                                           when
                    Hell will rule on Piedmont Street.

                    Ruin will prevail.

III

The last time Daniel spoke this sermon was much the same as the first, and he spoke it countless times because for some years now he had preached on Piedmont Street, walking it from one end to the other. His original suit became ragged and he grew thin in it. His shoes were cobbled with cardboard. His face often unshaven, his hair specked with lint. It was this derelict figure that grew familiar to the residents of the street.

Sometimes they loved him. Sometimes they mocked him. Some were frightened of him and crossed the street in avoidance. Rarely a person listened and sang out a response to his call.

"Do you hear me?"

"Yes, Preacherman. I hear you!"

Seasonal rains, violent and flooding rains, came yet still Daniel walked the street, preaching in the drenchings. A cough that took root in his chest finally went away, though long, long after the rains ended.

❖

He does not like to beg, but he will do it. On this morning a scowling middle-aged woman, a member of his daily congregation at the bus stop, slips her hand into her bag and pulls out a bill. She thrusts it at him, and in her gesture there is kindness and annoyance, pity and scorn. Daniel takes the dollar but he has no gratitude.

Why should he be thankful?

For he has left behind everything.

And has had to learn to live with loneliness. He has had to learn to relieve himself in alleys. When there's not enough money for a night, even an hour's stay in the transient hotels that have become his home, he has had to learn to sleep occasionally on a pavement in the chill or the heat.

And when he wakes to the breaking morning always he is being called.

So this is his life, to be a spectacle.

Singing, praising, clapping, stomping.

A glorious, mad spectacle, Daniel is.

IV

Yet the hour arrived when Daniel turned and looked at the old theater in its rasping, expiring state and he saw its disintegrating tower and, startled, he recognized it.

Because here was the thing. Daniel was different once.

Oh, the dandy in his youth, when his hair was black and parted with a thick line, his mustache trimmed, his mouth ruminating in perpetual motion with a paring of chewable tobacco, his nails manicured at the barbershop down the block, and adorning his little finger a diamond pinkie ring that was being paid off with usurious interest in installments.

"Hey, Daniel! It's Friday night!"

"I hear ya, Sonny. Nobody should be staying home on a Friday night."

Why waste another minute then? Get the evening started already! Sip a few drinks. Play a game of cards. And later catch the last show at King's.

King's! Now Daniel remembered.

At some time the theater had been new and grand (an elegant, ornate palace): and he had been part of its evening crowd (in his wallet his just-cashed pay from a week's worth of shifts at the bread factory). He bought his ticket, in the theater's packed lobby stepped on a toe ("Excuse me, Brother, I sincerely apologize"). Found a good enough seat (it was upholstered with velvet, or if not velvet then a material so similar that when his hand brushed against it to swipe away scattered kabooms of popcorn, he felt its creamy richness). Up ahead was the immense screen and loud, thrilled folk were every-where, thank goodness getting their money's worth. They sure knew how to have a good time. Daniel too threw his head back and laughed at the shenanigans. Because he could laugh in the days before he was called.

So he was different once! He remembered there was a woman seated beside him. She wore a flowery dress and rouge on her cheeks; she had scented herself with two-dollar perfume. And this woman was no stranger to him, not at all, and while her face was not beautiful her naked body was just fine and so Daniel had once known the joy of lust.

V

His calling came during the heat of Indian summer, his calling came during the storms of February. His calling came; incessantly, he has been called.

But on this day, not so long after Daniel remembered he had once been an ordinary and unburdened man, he tried one last time to avoid his calling. Yes, again Daniel was being called, yet he lay still and refused to open his eyes.

"Daniel," he heard over and over again, and finally in answer he whispered, "Please, Lord. Enough. Please let me be."

"Daniel."

So the preacherman pushed aside the thin cover and placed his feet on a gritty, unswept floor. He saw he was in a small wood-paneled room where he had been staying in fact for almost a month now. On the side of the bed he sat, his shoulders bare and muscled.

"Daniel, I'm calling you."

"Yes. Yes."

Daniel pushes himself up, washes his face and he dresses. And reflected in the cloudy mirror above the bathroom sink is a grizzled, pitiful figure. But why rail against what he's become? Why continue to weep? Why cuss and stomp?

Since there is no use fighting what one has been called to do. There is no use in resisting it.

So before he goes out to tell the residents of the street once again what they do not want to hear, Daniel prepares for himself a breakfast, a few eggs fried on a small griddle, a brewing pot of coffee. Meanwhile, he sets a tiny table with his plate and cup, an emptying sack of bread.

As before, the sounds of the birds have been replaced with the noise of traffic, and by this time Daniel is ready to eat.

Two matters he must attend to first, however; one is to sprinkle his eggs with hot sauce, the other to bow his head in a prayer of grace.

Teaching Pompeii
Mr. Stuyvesant

"The year was 79 A.D.," he said with a faded Dutch accent, "during the reign of Titus.

"Imagine the city of Pompeii awakening to a routine day. Perhaps not even a cloud in the sky to forecast doom.

"How were they to know the advent of peril? They could not, so they pursued their ordinary day."

He went on smoothly, his tone perhaps a little bored since he'd given this lecture many times before.

"Bakers putting bread into ovens. Shops opening for business. Children scrawling their lessons on wax tablets. Butchers slaughtering livestock. Prostitutes plying their trade."

The girls, all dark-haired and dressed in uniforms

of blue skirts and white blouses, grinned and giggled, as Mr. Stuyvesant knew they would. His own smile was broad, crooked, and charming.

Mr. Stuyvesant was the only male teacher in a girls' parochial school (not handsome and only of average height, balding yet masculine, fit; he was the object of many a crush) and history was his subject, especially European and ancient civilizations.

Behind him hung a map of the Roman Empire, doomed to fall by the semester's end. He pointed (a virile forearm revealed by short shirt-sleeves, tanned and downy) to the shoe of Italia's boot.

"Then Mount Vesuvius erupts!

"Lava flows. Ashes fall. Disaster comes to Pompeii."

One girl, whose name was Cecile, wrote, "The ashes swirled in a cruel, maiming blizzard, blinding the eyes, deafening the ears, choking the cries of its victims," which was not exactly what the teacher said.

"And not for another thousand years," he continued, "did excavators finally bring to the modern world the news of the ruins of Pompeii.

"Are there now any questions, ladies?"

There were none.

For homework Mr. Stuyvesant told them to finish reading the chapter. They also had algebra problems. And Sister Catherine had assigned their class to write a composition on the martyrs and saints, two elevated states of being they were too selfish and flawed, too ordinary in their ambitions to ever accomplish themselves.

Stucco Freestand
Mr. Clarence

Mr. Clarence was at work early, turning a vacant lot of broken glass and weeds into something worthwhile. What traffic there was turned on their headlights to cut through white-spun gossamer.

Fog is lonely, sad. Fog means a hot, hot day is coming, you know.

Already the foundation was poured and out of it poked two-by-fours like the ribs of a great whale. The day before the elderly operator of the shoeshine kiosk stiffly crossed the street and asked, "What kind of roof will it be? Red clay or shingle?"

"Shingle," Mr. Clarence had replied, and the elderly man stiffly crossed the street again. For the rest of the day he sat idly in his chair. His last known customers being a long time gone.

Mr. Clarence had a wife who felt superior to him; she discussed his shortcomings daily. And his sons warred openly on Piedmont Street.

Speaking of his sons, never had a single callus formed on either of their pairs of hands.

While Mr. Clarence's hands were brown with a blushed hue, like a rosy sky at dawn. His hands were large, double-jointed, and quite capable of building a stucco freestand with a plate-glass window and a neat perfect shingle roof. Perhaps he hoped most to be remembered in this way. And that it would stand for a long time; indeed, the forever he presumed was a long, long time.

As for now Mr. Clarence climbed the scaffold and he was thinking, Fog is lonely, sad. Fog means a hot, hot day is coming, you know.

House on Fire!
Mr. Wolcott

"House on fire!" was the shout and immediately people started coming from all directions.

Like pilgrimage.

Like streaming to a traveling show or carnival.

"House on fire!" a woman called out. She leaned from her opened window. Smell of fish frying wafted from inside and music was playing on the radio. House on fire! House on fire! were the lyrics.

A crowd by now was gathered, and latecomers grumbled that they were a mile away. A young boy sat on his daddy's strong shoulders. A lady wore pink slippers.

How'd it happen?

Somebody left the stove on again?

Child with matches?

Crazy, betrayed lover?

Flickering tips poked through the roof, which crumbled like a wafer of crackers. Flames punched out the windows and breathed fresh air while blackness roiled into a fine blue sky.

House on fire, it was a sight. People tilted their heads and gazed with interest, as they would to see if a great crane may drop its two-ton steel load.

House on fire! House on fire!

Soon enough there was nothing left except the brick chimney, which stood desolate and strangely sturdy.

Show's over. Let's go, somebody said.

Mr. Wolcott carried his son on his seemingly untiring shoulders, going back from where they came.

Before It Burned to the Ground
Cecile

Five years before it burned to the ground Cecile fell on a hard time (only temporary she was sure) and decided to get a loan on a valuable brooch. It was a moonstone brooch, very old, almost certainly an antique, given to her by her Auntie. Cecile had not loved the Auntie (apparently she would love seldom) but the brooch became a favorite. She pinned it frequently on the bolero jacket she was wearing right now as a matter of fact, unbuttoned because at the moment there was no wind. And although Cecile hated to give the moonstone brooch up, it was only for a short while, she told herself, just long enough to get through this hard time.

The pawnshop was on 3rd and Piedmont. Cecile had to first approach the misty atmosphere outside the

47

liquor store, so reeking that she shut her nostrils against it; therefore, each breath was swallowed hard and burning down her throat with the taste of beer. Men loitered there, they watched her walk by. Some of them, with their white hair and red, rheumy eyes, were old enough to be great-grandfathers, but it was the young one with the scruffy beard who made rude comment on her, saying, "So Miss High and Mighty in a rush. Everybody move out her way. Miss High and Mighty in a big hurry to get where she going."

Cecile didn't hear him. Beside the fact that the scruffy young man practically muttered the insult so low as to be hardly audible, she was already far down the block, her slightly pigeon-toed steps moving quite fast. Cecile was that determined to get to the pawnshop before closing.

And when she arrived there a bell above the lintel, an old-fashioned thing, sounded as she pushed open the door. It had a bent clapper so it announced her rather unceremoniously with a dull, clanking thud. (She did not notice how the gap from the opened door allowed in a shaft of late afternoon light, tangerine-imbued.)

Instead her attention focused immediately on the fact that there was a long line (she took her place at the end). Therefore, other people must have fallen on a hard time too, she supposed, but insisted once again, "Of course mine will be only temporary."

So why should she be ashamed?

Since she had tried, she had tried to call them Honey and Sweethearts and tried to tell them that a whole note equals four counts, a quarter note is one; she had tried to remind them (Cutie Pies, Dearhearts, Brats) of the sharp notes of Beautiful Dreamer when they only wanted to play that silly Heart and Soul, to *Curve your fing-ers as you play, that's the on-ly, on-ly way; Count out loud and keep the beat. Ma-king music is a treat* [1] in that tiny Piedmont Street storefront that had the nerve to call itself a music school; she had tried not to call them stupid because then they cried and never came back despite their fierce mothers owing for three weeks of lessons — three weeks without paying!

Wait.

Someone was shouting.

---

1 From *Beginning the Keyboard: A Piano Primer* by David Carr Glover: Chas H. Hansen Music Corp., NY 1969

———

Gradually, quite gradually Cecile had been coming to realize that at the head of the line a pint-sized man was shouting. "Motherfuckit! Motherfuckit!" he was shouting. "HellGoddamnMotherfuckitall!" Meanwhile the Pawnbroker was on the other side of the counter, perhaps sitting on a stool. When Cecile stood on tiptoes and peered past the shoulder in front of her, she could see this, and also that the Pawnbroker's elbow was braced on the counter surface, and his cheek rested on the leaned shelf of his palm.

"Take it or leave it," she heard the Pawnbroker say in a quiet, normal voice, and the small furious man, at once subdued, answered bitterly, "I'll take it then."

Now the door was opening again (and again the antique bell with the damaged clapper remarked a dull listless clank offensive to the ear). And this time Cecile did not notice the shaft of strong late afternoon light casting upon a copper teapot on the shelf, making it seem almost like treasure, wildly, frantically glittering as fool's gold does. When the door shut, the light vanished, the teapot was again ordinary, and now inside the store stood a man carrying a chandelier.

Time being it took a while but the dawning came to Cecile, just as the man winked in response to her stare, that some innocent party now had an unsolicited hole in the roof of his house.

In Cecile's own hand was held the moonstone brooch. She was admiring it, there in her palm, a milky oval clasped in a setting of white gold. Cecile was a child when she received it as a present and it was her regret now that perhaps she had not been grateful enough to her Auntie at the time. Well, she was grateful now. The pin should be worth a lot of money, for hadn't Auntie always let you know the value of her gifts? Yes, it should bring in more than enough money to get Cecile through this hard time, which would certainly only be of short duration, Cecile was convinced, and if Auntie was not dead and buried in Piedmont Cemetery she would thank her profusely; so again why should she feel ashamed? She had tried, she had tried. She had tried to prompt them (Buttercups, Cherubs, Monsters) to *Count, sing, name the notes. While your fing-ers play*[2]; she'd tried to tell them that allegro means to hurry, hurry; and she'd tried to teach them the staccato beats of the marches, the rests of waltzes, and how to turn a light, prancing touch of the piano keys into a shower of rain. She had tried, she was trying, she was trying...

Oh, apparently her turn had finally come. Cecile heard the word "next" and found herself stepping to the counter. And that's when she saw the Pawnbroker's face was snow, it was snow and ice — when this was a landscape that was ruled by the sun and its hard, forceful presence; other faces were toasted and roasted by it, crimsoned and burnt. But his face was snow. It was ice. His white, white hair a snowy bank sloping across a blanched forehead.

She placed the brooch on the counter.

"It's moonstone," she said.

"Is that so?" he answered, for the first time looking straight at her. (And she found out that his eyes were grey, like the skies in winter countries, and from such

---

2 *Beginning the Keyboard*, Glover

skies, Cecile knew, snow falls. Meanwhile the Pawnbroker saw that Cecile's eyes were a loamy brown and that her hair was pinned high in a cluster of curls. But he did not allow these observations to interfere with the way things must operate.)

So without even a need to clear his throat he went ahead and named his price.

"How much?" Cecile asked.

The Pawnbroker repeated himself.

After that was a hesitation on Cecile's part. It gave the Pawnbroker enough time to scratch to satisfaction an itch on his neck. He was done before she was, so he gave her a nudge by saying, "It's no heirloom, you know. It's just a trinket."

Again Cecile hesitated, this time with a tilt of her head that directed her gaze upward, bringing into her startled view the suspended instruments — horns and guitars and drums — that dangled from wires fixed to the ceiling. With her head posed like that, it almost appeared she was listening to a tune they were playing; yet in actuality it was a most eerily silent orchestra, and as a result the rest of the transaction would take place beneath this mute symphony, as mute as the heavens can be in answer to prayer.

"All right," Cecile said, and to herself she added, This is the way of the world. *PART I: Cecile's story.*

In *PART II* of Cecile's story she sits on a bench at a bus stop where she counts the money, and each time she counts it it is still not enough; however, it will have to do.

It will have to do until things get better, Cecile told herself. And on that not-too-distant day she will go back to the pawnshop to retrieve her brooch and pin it once again on the lapel of the bolero jacket she was just now buttoning against the mild wind that had begun to blow from the west, slightly at first but increasing in strength, to signal that evening was coming. Cecile turned into it and without notice or appreciation felt its refreshment on her cheeks. In this way she saw looming over the incline the #54 bus.

In a hurry now she put the yellow pawn ticket she would one better day redeem and the money that wasn't enough but would have to do into a red

Chinese silk wallet that she then dropped into her purse.

PART III: The bus was very crowded and so Cecile stood in its packed aisle. She held on to a metal pole that served as her center of gravity. Right under her nose sat a young mother with a sleeping infant on her lap. Sweet innocent baby, sweet pure little baby, was Cecile's rather bitter thought.

And the dingy landscape of Piedmont Street slid by, ruled by the sun. Snow never falls here, she thought. Snow falls in winter countries. And ashes, she remembered, fell in Pompeii.

Well, well, the money would have to do. But why did the Pawnbroker say that the brooch was worth practically nothing? This brooch that was carved of the gleaming marble of the moon. This brooch which was made of the translucent moon and had been given to her by her Auntie who had made it sound like such a treasure, an invaluable gem, the stuff of fortunes.

Ha! Cecile gave a harsh laugh. (Other bus passengers darted their eyes to keep watch on her.)

How do you like that, Auntie! (But she was still dead and buried in Piedmont Cemetery and so could not answer.) He said the brooch was a trinket!

And now the sweet innocent baby was waking, stretching its tiny mouth. Little warning to prepare one's self for child wails with plumes.

PART IV: Because this was the world, the world, the world. This was the world, and the Pawnbroker understood the way of the world, that a brooch lovely and precious as the moon was not worth much. Here Cecile tried to remember, did we even exchange the barest of courtesies? Did we greet one another? —HOW ARE YOU? —FINE, AND YOURSELF? —DOING WELL, THANK YOU. Or, a perfunctory comment on the weather? —NOT A CLOUD IN THE SKY. IT'S BEEN A LONG WHILE SINCE THE LAST TIME IT RAINED. —THE FORE-CAST SAYS DROUGHT. —OH, Cecile would have exclaimed to that, HOW AWFUL FOR THE ROSE BUSHES.

No, they got right to the business of it. The business of it being that Cecile, she was certain, had been cheated of the true value of the brooch. It was the way of the world, and the Pawnbroker knew the way of the world. In his eyes, the color of a winter sky, snow fell, ashes fell.

PART V: And this money will just have to do.

PART VI: The bus stopped but that's not when it happened. People got off, on. Somebody stepped on Cecile's toes, but that's not when it happened either. She shifted her hips and redistributed her weight. Her feet were aching but she barely recognized that fact. The bus lurched and with grinding gears set off again.

PART VII: And now as the bus traveled it happened, when Cecile, who was not truly meant for this world, who was bound to be spotted by every keen-eyed hawk, every fork-tongued reptile, every lowdown skunk, every wolf in sheep's clothing, was in a swirl of snowflakes and ashes; and so easily and foolishly seduced, Cecile thought she imagined a presence. A pleasant sniff of a perspiring stink. An almost imperceptible tickle of her ear. A glimpse of snakeskin shoes. *Oh, she was so recklessly, eagerly tempted and seduced.* The feel of a phantom breath on the back of her neck. (Her hair was pinned in a cluster of curls): and she felt his breath on her bare, exposed nape.

His breath on her nape! Cecile's eyes widened.

There'd been no jolt, no bump.

Really nothing more substantial yet informative than intuition. The tears in Cecile's eyes miraculously balanced themselves and she did not even turn around.

PART VIII: As soon as Cecile stepped off the bus she searched her purse. Rummaging and rummaging, eventually without panic or hope, she examined the purse to its dusky lining. Although it was already proven and unalterable that her red Chinese silk wallet with the money that was not enough and the yellow pawn ticket she meant one day to redeem was gone.

PART IX: With a glance up, Cecile saw the streetwoman but stubbornly refused to believe in her existence. Yet the vision persisted. Of course the woman was crazy, but aside from that little else was absolute, if she was old or young, fat or thin. One thing, however, though now in tatters the dress she wore had once been a ballroom gown. (So perhaps like the street itself she had known better days.) It had a velvet bodice and lace sleeves; it had a torn gathered skirt which the streetwoman lifted to piss on the ground.

And if there was a blush at her disgrace, it did not bleed through the plum-black of her cheeks.

PART X and *FINAL INSTALLMENT:* It is an hour before it burns to the ground and things have not gotten better; in fact, they've gone much worse. Cecile returns to the pawnshop (again the bell with the bent clapper; again the late-afternoon tangerine-hued sunlight striking the copper teapot; again the instruments above head, silent as heaven).

In clasped hands Cecile holds a rare yellow butterfly that should be quite valuable. But when she unfolds her palms, to her amazement, there is nothing.

❖

So, she thought, I am the luckless, the incompetent, the broken, the lost. Mr. Pawnbroker! I am your clientele; I am your daily bread. And oh, what a stupid man you are! What a fool! Yes, a fool!

Because you have chosen the occupation that leads to this meeting with me. And I will turn on you. I will turn on you. It'll be your own fault when it happens.

At my command, that cowardly door will buckle and splinter. And I will burst through with the force of a crowd. Tumbling in with empty hands and flat pockets. But on exit I will carry bicycles and trombones and crystal candlesticks.

I myself will pour the gasoline. Soon the air will choke.

And mercy I may show. Or mercy I may not.

Oh, Mr. Pawnbroker, what a risk you take. Your face is snow. Your face is ice. Sun melts snow. Fire thaws ice. And then what will you be but a puddle on the ground? For a thirsty stray dog to come along and lap you up.

❖

All this time not another customer has entered the shop.

The Pawnbroker looks at Cecile and she at him. In his eyes snow and ashes fall.

In her eyes flare a strange wildness.

In her eyes, which are a loamy brown, sprout stalks of bird of paradise, bright and aflame as torches.

Vivian

Vivian dreams of fire. She dreams of orange flames heating the temperature of the night. Night black night is best for dreaming.

Full moon risen so bright, the window shade half-drawn against it. In its strong light, the night turns vague and atmospheric; roses on the wallpaper incarnate and revealed as Vivian's boldness; her naked body uncovered by washed bleached sheets.

(Men dream of Vivian dreaming of fire. Men who too grow restless on a night made hot by her dreaming.)

She is dreaming of fire. She is dreaming of sky-high flames.

Humidity dews her upper lip.

Bracelet sears gold into flesh.

Scorching to any wayward tongue.

Where
It Burned to the Ground

Red Lipstick
Albee & Lettie

Lettie's coming.

She's coming. On her way. To Piedmont Street, she's coming.

That was her calling on the telephone. Telling me she'll be here soon.

Lettie.

Jesus Lord. So much to do.

"Who is this?" I said. "Who?" My voice was harsh, not like me at all. That ringing phone had pulled me from my bed, that's how early it was, and I'm up by seven every morning. It's been that way for years. "Who?"

"Albee?" she said. I didn't know her voice. Imagine that. She spoke again, this time adding a weight to her words, leveling her tone with authority, calm.

"Albertine."

"Lettie."

Lettie. Lettie. Lettie. Her name rolls along my mind like a prayer, a curse. Like the sing-song of a children's nursery rhyme, a chant to jump rope by: Here comes Lettie. Here she comes. Lettie. Lettie. My best-best friend. Lettie. Lettie. The one I loved. Oh, but that was a long time ago.

On her way back to me at last. I stood in the hallway after we hung up, wearing just a nightgown, my feet bare against the hallway floor, bumps on my arms and the back of my neck, a chill I was feeling and at the same time not feeling. I was bound to get sick, I was thinking, in spite of flu shots. Nothing would save me. Such strange thoughts. About my heart, leaping so against my chest. It would jump out, I was certain, and I crossed my arms, trying to hold it back. All these bits jumbled inside me. Until I couldn't think at all, like the times now I am driving and suddenly people honk their horns at me, an ugly, rude chorus, when I have no idea what wrong I have done, making me stop in my tracks, same as the little brown rabbit startled in the woods, black eyes bright and body stiff, stopped in the middle of the intersection and so nobody can go until I'm able to breathe again.

I have to reach for breath after Lettie calls. The weight of my crossed arms squeezed against my breasts. What a sight I would make for the woman doctor who worries about my blood pressure. Until I begin to rub my arms, my cheeks, the still rabbit coming back to life. Lettie's on her way, and I have to prepare.

First move I make is to pull on my old housedress with the green and brown and yellow checkered squares, torn and stitched with safety pins beneath the right arm. Tie a kerchief around my head on the way to the front yard, the first sight that will greet Lettie. I carry the broom for sweeping the curb where dirt and slips of paper and soda cans have collected. But first the lawn. Down on my hands and knees, my eyes narrowed and searching the grass for weeds, I crawl about, snatching at dandelions and crabgrass until green streaks stain my palms. When the walk catches my sight. My new walk that Mr. James in the green house on the corner just finished building without taking a penny. Mr. James with

69

his pretty wife who nudges him to help the old widow down the street. He laid the walk just the way I asked, with bricks of different colors — pink, of course, but also coral and burgundy, yellow and green and grey. Like a crazy quilt, that's what I told him. Like Joseph's coat.

I squeeze my eyes tight and see Lettie strolling along the new walk. The way she was years ago, wearing one of her dresses, bright-colored and the skirt swinging, brushing the back of her knees. Her plump cheeks and the skin the shade of black plums. Her hats — the straw one with the scarves tied around the brim, the tails drifting down her back, and that man's hat tilted on her head, shadowing one eye. I see her hair dyed yellow. (How my Harald talked her down for that! "A woman with skin that black," he said, like it was some crime. "She's got no business.") I see tripled strands of fake pearls slapping against her breasts as she stepped, and her lips, slick and shiny red, open and stretched across laughing teeth.

"Miz Clark?" I hear, and open my eyes. Sonya from across the street stands on my lawn. "Miz Clark?" She says. They all call me that. "How you doing today,

Miz Clark?" they say, "You getting along all right, Miz Clark?" No longer Albertine. Nobody remembers Albertine but me. "Miz Clark?" Sonya is saying. "You doing O.K., Miz Clark?" Her little boy and girl dressed in blue uniforms, on their way to the Christian school. They hold Sonya's hands and stare at me with dark brown eyes, the girl's hair all in braids and fastened with blue-and-white barrettes.

"You've been working hard," Sonya says. "I saw you." Her voice is weak, surprising because Sonya's a big woman. A big yellow woman. The way she fusses at me is how I imagine a daughter would, and I know I should be thankful for neighbors like her. "Maybe you should rest," she says, but I grin and pat her fleshy arm. Tell her to stop worrying. That's all I say. She wouldn't understand the rest, that I haven't felt so good in a long, long time.

Lettie never said what she wanted when she called. But I know. The same as how I know almost everything about Lettie. More, probably, than in those days we talked all the time. I know about that new house of hers and how each of her daughters turned out, about each wedding, each birth of a grandchild, each baptism, communion, graduation. I know about her boy, her baby. How his motorbike skidded on an oil-slicked road. He was nearly killed and I know that nearly killed her. There are people who tell me these things. Essie in particular, but sometimes I wonder if I need them. I feel I would know no matter what. I would just know.

"Can I come over today, Albee?" she said. "I've got something to ask you." What answer possible, except "Of course, Lettie." All this time her words swirling in my mind until, finally, while working in the yard their meaning comes to me, makes me sit back on my heels although this causes great pain in my legs. Already my palms sting, my back hurts from all the pulling and stooping but I have taken certain pleasure in all these aches, accepted any suffering stemming from Lettie's visit as natural and expected. Now at this moment, I don't feel a thing. "So that's what she wants," I say, then snap my mouth shut, in case Sonya's back across the street, watching.

There's sickness eating through Lettie, Essie told

me. She says it can't be fought. "They put her in the hospital time after time," Essie said. "But she always comes out." I could picture Essie on the other end of the telephone, shaking her head, rust-colored curls trembling. But I know better. Lettie is a cat. What else Essie tells me, that Lettie's alone. "Alonso's left her," she lowered her voice when she told me this, and on my end of the phone I nodded my head. My whole body nodding, my shoulders rocking back and forth, my toes in it too, tapping the floor. Ah, Alonso. Couldn't take any more. Lettie's carryings-on and her lies. Her arrogance. See there. I'm not the only one. "And the children," Essie said. "All gone too." That boy turned out no better than her. Traipsing around the country. Living with one woman after another. The twins, Claire and Carla. "They won't have nothing to do with her." Essie's tone hushed. Gleeful. "Won't even let her in their homes."

"It's payment due," I said. "Fortune's wheel turning round. All Lettie's deeds coming back to her. All the evil, all the lies, all the boozing, all her selfishness. All the suffering she's caused." I had to catch myself, listen to Essie's silence. It made me press my lips tight. Nobody wants to hear me talk that way.

Alone. That's why Lettie's coming back. She needs my help.

She'll be here soon, and so I move inside to the living room. She'll only pass through here, Lettie and I were never living-room friends. Still I take my old dust rags and wipe the Beethoven bust on the piano. I grip the bench and lower myself one knee at a time to clean the instrument's feet, pushing my fingernail through the cloth to get at the dust in the carved ridges. I pour lemon oil on the coffee table and knead it into the wood. The centerpiece is an arrangement of silk-screen flowers. It would be nice to replace it with a token from Lettie, but there is nothing. A punch bowl that Harald dropped years ago. When we were children I'd give Lettie presents. Little bracelets with dangling charms and necklaces with mustard seeds captured in glass balls. I stole from my mother's jewelry box a pin shaped like a bird with rhinestones on its breast. Lettie and I believed they were diamonds. How Mama whipped me when she found out. I gave Lettie the toy circus animals my daddy bought me when I was sick with chicken pox. Tiny, tiny things. When I shut my eyes now I can see them still: a lion, a monkey, a capped bear holding a little red ball. Lettie won't remember.

In the kitchen I fill a bucket with ammonia and hot water, sink my bare hands in and swirl the rag about. My fingers look strange, puffy, bloated, plain except for the wedding band I still wear though Harald's been gone, what?, almost ten years. In the moment it takes to squeeze the rag my hands have turned a raw red. I was the fair-skinned one with the pretty hair. Lettie standing in the schoolyard behind me, playing with my ponytail, saying, "This is good stuff." Combing it with her fingers, plaiting it, dressing it with ribbons. She chose me, I remind myself as I clean. "Me." Wiping down the windowsill above the sink where I keep my pot of violets, the ceramic swan with the white, curved neck, the goldfish bowl. Harald's glasses. The last pair he owned, cracked in the brown frame. Oh, Harald never liked Lettie. He saw before I did. The way his face would turn mean at the sight of her children here. But

I didn't mind taking care of them, I tried to tell him, since we couldn't have any of our own. "Fool," he said. He knew what Lettie was doing, how she got those fancy hats and bottles of perfume cluttering her glass-topped vanity. "Fool," he said, and I thought he meant Alonso.

I want Lettie to see those glasses. And the drawings held by magnets to the refrigerator. Sonya's children colored those and signed them with love and kisses. I want Lettie to take note of the cabinets beneath the sink; Mr. James built those, yes, the same one who did the walk. And the large bowl on the table, let her see that too, filled with figs and oranges and lemons and tomatoes and yellow squash. My neighbors pick these from their trees and gardens and carry them over in oil-stained paper bags. All this will show Lettie. "See, I have friends. See what my friends do for me. Lettie? Do you hear? I have a good life. I keep busy. I substitute-teach and lunch twice a month with Essie. I attend all the meetings of the neighborhood block club, elected secretary two years in a row."

I shake my head. Standing in the middle of my kitchen, hands on hips, the rag dripping ammonia-water on the floor. I have no time for this, there is much more to do. A new fresh tablecloth and the good curtains, yellow ones that will match my kitchen, I need to get them down from the hall cabinet. I will fix tuna sandwiches, cut in triangles and trimmed of crusts, just how she likes, and put the rest of the coconut cake on the party platter with the red and yellow tulips decorating the border. When Lettie comes I will put on a pot of coffee. We used to sit at this very table and drink cup after cup. Lettie making me laugh. If I had more time I would get on hands and knees and scrub the floor. I would wipe down the cabinet doors, the woodwork, the walls till free of fingerprints and grime and grease. Sort through the cupboards, throw out the clutter, the excesses, and reline the shelves with fresh, new paper. I would clean this house to its bones, its soul. I would cook Lettie her favorite meal, gumbo with sausage and crab and shrimp. All that and more if I had the time. But a million years would not be enough to prepare for Lettie.

It's remarkable to me that I didn't know her voice. Of course it's been several years since we spoke on the telephone or anywhere else. But that doesn't mean I had stopped hearing Lettie. No, I've heard her voice often. Still it follows me around, sits on my shoulder and whispers in my ear, pops up at the strangest times. Once when I was slicing eggplant and something about it, its deep black purpleness, I think, like Lettie's color, made me think of her and I swear I heard her laughing. Another time I was humming some nonsense tune I made up as I leaned over the back-porch sink washing my clothes and her voice rose up over mine, singing one of those common, nasty songs she used to know. I must hear her in my sleep too, because sometimes I wake in the night answering her.

Something to ask me, that's what she said, and that is just like Lettie. Seems like she was always wanting something from me. Never the other way around. Didn't Harald say that? And Essie? Oh, I was a good friend to her, everybody knows that. But I've learned my lesson now. I'm stronger than before. "Where are my little toy animals now?" My voice bounces against the tile walls of the bathroom. I hear in it the frantic pain of the old crazy woman filthily dressed who stands at the bus stop and shouts all her business. With trembling fingers I unbutton my old plaid dress and soap a washcloth to rub against the back of my neck, my ears, beneath my arms. Fill the basin with water and bring my face down.

People wondered after I let Lettie go. Prying, nudging questions. Essie tried to find out, oh, how she tried. She was so certain it was some one, huge thing. She questioned me about Lettie and my Harald; she knew how Lettie was. But I never answered. Let Essie think whatever she wants, tell her tales. But this is how Lettie and I came to an end.

The Christmas party at Essie's house and me still in my widow's black although Harald had been gone more than two years. That's how deeply I felt, Lettie should have known that. At this party I was sitting on Essie's flowered couch, a paper plate on my lap, listening to Chloe. I was eating one of those big black olives, nodding my head to whatever talk she was talking when I heard Lettie's voice coming from the kitchen (who did not hear?) saying, "No, I don't think it's time Albertine stopped wearing black. Black suits Albertine." And then she laughed. I heard her laugh.

I went home after that and took off that black dress. I sat on my bed dressed only in my slip, my arms folded against the chilled night air, and began to think about Lettie and me. I combed through our history together.

Pulling memories like loose threads. One for the time after my third miscarriage when Lettie said to me, "Obviously the Lord doesn't intend for you to have babies, Albertine. Not every woman is meant to be a mother." A thread for the time creditors were after me, when I could have lost this home Harald and I worked so hard for (and I'll let you know I never asked for a dime) and Lettie's answer: "Every top must stand on its own bottom." Another for those two days Harald stayed in the hospital, those terrible last days, and she never came. Every insult, every hurt, every slight since childhood. All thought forgotten or excused or forgiven. All that I had chosen not to see. I sat there in the dark with goosebumps on my bare arms, pulling them from a place deep within me, weaving these threads together. Lettie had never been my friend. She had never loved me as I loved her.

The face I wash is old and full, skin loose and drooping beneath the chin, at the neck. Never have I been one of those women to worry about vanity and I do not try to hide my age now. I pat on a little bit of powder and line my mouth with lipstick, pale pink, not red like Lettie. Once, foolishly, I asked Essie, "Does she ever mention me?" Anything would have pleased me, even spiteful words. "Does she?" And Essie waited, I could hear her thoughts, weighing whether to spare me, before answering what I knew to be true. "No," she said. "Not once." I hold my brush with tight, curled fingers. My knuckles hurt. Twist my hair and pin it in two tightly wound coils.

At the closet I fumble through my hanging dresses. Which one? The black dress with the white polka dots? No. Eh heh. Nothing black today. The green one? The striped one? None of them seems right.

Lettie will show up here in something red, hem swinging, slapping. She'll wear a hat with a feather sprouting out, or the brim trimmed with fur. Strutting up my walk without shame.

I could say no. That would serve her right. Laugh at Lettie when she asks for my help. Like she would do me. Leave her deserted. Yes. Exactly what I should do.

Such unchristian thoughts ruling my mind as I stand before the closet. Finally, I shake my head and get back to business. It's the striped dress I finally choose.

Getting time now. She'll be here. Here. I rush over to press my dress, scorching my arm below the wrist. A bad burn, but the hurt will come later. For now I am free. Standing next to the ironing board, it takes long minutes to button up that dress. Lettie.

Sometime past two o'clock I wrap the sandwiches in wax paper and push the plate far back in the refrigerator. Cover the cake and set it back on the counter. She should have been here two hours ago. Just like Lettie. To keep me waiting. And then I realize, such a horrible thought it makes me sink into one of the kitchen chairs. I brace my elbows against the table. She's not coming.

Has nothing changed?

I hear her first. Jump up and run to the window with loud thudding steps that shake the floor, stand behind the sheer yellow curtains. Lettie's here. That's her car. The gold Cadillac. I remember how she fussed and nagged until Alonso bought it though they barely had money enough for a house to live in. I step back from the window, clap my hands, lift my feet and turn in a circle. I have to do something with all this feeling bouncing inside me. "Lettie," I sing.

Does she ever think of the time she took me to the beach? I watched through the window that day too when she drove up in the Cadillac, new and gleaming then. "Let's go somewhere," she said, and I tugged the kerchief from my head. We drove, little Alonso not even born yet and the twins mere toddlers, fussing in the back seat, nearly two hours along the coast to a mission town. Lettie wearing her straw hat that time with a yellow scarf tied around the brim, the tail fluttering out the window. We came to a beach with the prettiest, clearest water I've ever seen, white pebbles that hurt my stocking feet.

Lettie left us behind, her two babies and me, to climb the rocks. She found herself a place to settle, her straight black skirt pulled up, showing her thighs, and a bottle of orange pop in one hand. Her hair was still colored yellow then. Harald was right: a common-looking false blonde. I remember the babies crawling over my stomach, their reaching, slapping hands in my face struggling for attention, when all I wanted was to stare at Lettie sitting so bold on her rock. Not seeing us at all. And I was thinking, "We ought to take these babies, Harald and me. Away from her. Raise them right." Treacherous thoughts, not like me at all, and I tried to shrug them off, a burdensome cloak around my shoulders, heavy, anchoring me. "We could run into the ocean," I whispered to those babies, gathered in my arms. "Disappear. Drown. She'd never know." And though it was hard I waited and waited until it seemed enough time had passed so I could stand and call to her, wave her back to us, shouting, "Lettie. Lettie. Let's go home."

All the times I have remembered that day and what warning I should have taken. But I've learned. I won't be a fool again.

I hurry back to the window. "It's her. Lettie." On Piedmont Street. Starting up my new walk. "What will she say about that?" I whisper. "My walk of different colors? About my dress? What cruel things?"

And then I see her. I see Lettie.

She's got skinny. Too skinny. Oh, that's a bad skinny.

I step close to the window, my face pressed into the curtains. Where is her hat? She wears a wig, a cheap one, too obvious; it is brown with strands thick and straight as a horse's mane. She wears a black dress.

Black!

Lettie is dying.

Essie was right, I can see that now. This sickness has defeated her and now me too. Robbed me of my Lettie. Left me empty-handed. What business have I got against this woman here? I leave the window, don't want to see anymore. Betrayed again.

Racing all around my kitchen, the nervous little brown rabbit. All the things that should give me comfort. I reach and take Harald's glasses from the windowsill, hold them to my lips. But from them get nothing. No power. Compared to Lettie it's worthless. Everything in my pretty yellow kitchen, worthless.

So I walk back to the window and push the curtains aside. A ghost stands on my front porch, and inside myself I feel something falling. Falling.

"Lettie." Her name leaves my mouth in a wail. It carries through the glass pane and causes her to look my way. Through the window our eyes meet. Startled eyes, wondering, watchful. And then I see, what I have been searching for all along. Her red lips. Red. Red. Nothing but red. Oh, Lettie's always worn the brightest red lipstick, ever since she was a girl and her mother couldn't slap her into stopping. *See there. Not yet. Why, I'd bet anything, beneath that wig she still dyes her hair blonde. Scarce, nappy, yellow hairs. I'd bet my life.*

I let go the curtain, fall back and lean myself against the wall. Breathless.

She will ask me for this favor. I know it, and without hesitation I will answer. Yes. Always yes. Anything to keep Lettie near.

86

And I begin to imagine the caring of Lettie. Shopping in the market, picking out the finest okra, the best green beans. For her. Plaiting Lettie's hair, pinning it up at night so she can sleep in comfort. Peeling potatoes to simmer in a stew to feed her. Washing her soiled underclothes. Bathing her, soaping and scrubbing her pathetic, racked limbs. Sitting by her bedside, squeezing her hand when she cries out in pain.

All these visions bring me joy. My victory.

Now I stand in the middle of my kitchen, alone on the checkered tile floor, and listen to the doorbell ring. Twice more I hear it, dainty and distant, but still I have trouble moving. Finally, after what seems an instant, what feels my lifetime, I take my first steps. On my way toward greeting Lettie.

Piedmont Street
Bonita's Song

I remember when it was a nice street, once upon a time, all that jazz, so on and so forth. Once the street was young and handsome. Once the street was calcium-boned and luster-skinned. Once the street had money in its pockets.

Now look at what it's become:

Now the street wets its pants and scratches its itchy head.

Now the street gets high and stumbles clownishly.

Now the street rambles incoherently and laughs with odd timing.

Now the street holds out its jaundiced palm for spare change.

With the soft light of dawn materializes a woman prostitute, like a steep, unclimbable cliff.

We don't see her harbinger because the street is still young and handsome, calcium-boned and luster-skinned.

Yet, does she sing? Does she sing? Does she sing?

If so her voice is rough-hewn and splintered, and we may faintly hear her songs.

Sometimes cruel and dirty, but once in a while they sound like this:

> All childhoods are sweet bliss,
>> Though sad, sad, some too soon ending.

> The treetops blossom,
>> Jacaranda and callistemon.
> Out come flapping the cawing crows,
>> Dressed in black.
>> Oh, dressed in black.

> They ground their feet.
> Hands from hiding slip out of dark

Sleeves.

And carry prayer books and rosaries.

All childhoods are sweet bliss.

Though sad, sad, some

    Too soon ending.

Piedmont Street Cemetery

These days the dead stay buried. No longer do they get up like they did in the old days to bother decent folks. Years past one may have followed you around, given you the shivers. Or a dead husband may have visited his old bed and wife.

But these days they stay dead and buried in the Piedmont Street Cemetery. And they converse only with themselves.

The Bird of Paradise
(Of the Botanical Genus *stre-LIT-zia*)

The Bird of Paradise, also known as the Crane Flower, is a favorite for our gardens. The perfectly formed flower really does resemble a beautiful, strange bird; and it brings to my mind an ornamentation grandly marking the hat of a woman on her way to Sunday prayer service.

On Piedmont Street, *S. reginae* is the variety I have found to have the most prevalent presence; it could be considered too familiar and common, almost a weed.

As a plant it is tough, waxy, resilient, surviving even lengthy years of drought, which is every so often the climate of this locale.

But the Bird of Paradise is also ideal for moist, tropical places as rain — especially a wild, turbulent, destructive storm — seems to inspire its joyous and gaudy vanity.

Colorful and undemure, in fact brazen, striking, this species is recognizable by igneous orange petals (almost the blossom scorches one's hand) which brightly consume sparse tongues of blue.

One last point, and that is the irony of its name.

From *An Unofficial Guide to Our Neighborhood Plants and Flowers* by an anonymous author

In this place there
are rains and
drought
and plagues of termites.

The Official History of Piedmont Street
Elliot J. Piedmont

Once there was no street at all. Just an ungraded dirt path which posed a formidable challenge, whatever the season. In summer pedestrians were likely to sink ankle-deep in dust; in winter it was mud; on windy days, clouds of sand nearly suffocated man and beast alike; and in the rainy months stagnant pools of water and seas of mud made it almost impossible to cross from one side to the other. Beyond that, mudholes large enough to drown a man or mire a ten-mule team vied with piles of asphalt, dirt, and bricks to trap a journeying horseman. Old boots and shoes, fruits and vegetables, and animal carcasses were among the debris that made traveling the street a challenge.

Indeed, a street like ours starts humble enough —

its sidewalks rudimentary, packed dirt curbed with boards, and crowded with bootblack stands, fruit peddlers, patent-remedy hawkers. Newcomers come streaming across the limits, enticed by promises of Paradise, fig trees, and happiness. Soon enough a city begins to form, "charged with the responsibility of making improvement for the public use." And along with that come soil evaluations, chalk measurements, systems of drainage, public meetings, construction bids, and eventually hospitals and schools, houses of worship, libraries and banks and factories.

Naturally, part of the process is the naming of our public thoroughfares.

Yes, of course, a street must be named.

You who traverse our municipal arterials, have you given a thought to that? A street must be named. And perhaps you have wondered, from where do our city roads derive their titles?

It is an interesting question to pose.

And the broad and comprehensive answer is, from:

A) CITRUS, TREES, HERBS, AS WELL AS OTHER FORMS OF VEGETATION: Check any city map and what are you assured to find? An Oak Street or Oakwood or Acorn, that's what. Also a Cypress Avenue, a Eucalyptus Lane and Pine Crest Drive. How about the floral names of Heliotrope or Jasmine? Or the sweetly monikered Rose Street? In addition, you may spot a Basil Street, or Maplewood and Lemon Avenues.

B) VIEWS AND TERRAINS: An abundance of city street names exists under this heading, including Fairview, Prospect, Vantage, Viewpark, Craggy View and Picturesque Drive. One must also count High Hill, High Knoll, Cliff Drive, Rolling and Ravine Roads as well as Hidden Trail Lane.

C) BIRDS: Surely you have come across a Lark Court or a Falcon Place? A Crane Boulevard or Quail Drive? Or perhaps you have made your way along an Eagle Street. And if not that, then a Swallow Lane.

D) FOREIGN CITIES, PROVINCES, ISLANDS, AND COASTS: Possibly these names reflect homesickness or a yen for the exotic for among these streets are found Antigua Road, Chile Street, a Lisbon Lane, and Majorca Place.

E) A GENERAL SENSE OF DIRECTION AND ENUMERATION: Unimaginative, certainly, but here you will find North Street, South Street, East and West Streets, and Central Avenue. Also encompassed is 1st, 2nd, 3rd, 4th, and so on and so on.

F) MISCELLANEOUS, HEROES AND GEMS: Now we reach an eclectic heading, for a street name may be inspired by a storybook hero Aladdin, or to honor universities or saints or mythic gods of fire and wind and battle. Streets may derive their names from gems (Amethyst Street, Quartz Avenue, Emerald Drive, Pearl Place) or follow themes of stars (Starlight Drive, Stardust Place), the sun (Sundial Lane, Sunlight Place, Sunset Court), or the moon (Mooncrest Drive, Moonblind Avenue, Moonbeam Lane).

———

Our particular street falls into a grouping of CIVIC LEADERS, COMMUNITY BOOSTERS, and ILK: This is a heading which includes judges and bankers and ministers, vigilantes and sheriffs, governors, silver miners, wharf and railroad builders, headmistresses and chancellors, as well as generals and philanthropists. For those who may be interested, a book listing these august forebears and their accomplishments may be discovered in the city library, for outstanding citizens like to keep record of themselves for posterity. Unfortunately, these are tomes rarely checked out. (Yes, a very sad fate for a book to be considered obsolete, to be neglected.) And almost all of their subjects have been long out of mind.

But among the important pages of such a document can be found the biography of Elliot J. Piedmont, since it is he who received the honor of having our street bear his name.

Born in 1848, he was the son of Croydon and Lucy W. (Hutchison) Piedmont. He was tall, lean, and bespectacled due to nearsightedness. Perhaps an odd and trivial detail to record about him, it was noted that every hair on his head had turned white by the age of twenty-five.

As a young lawyer, Elliot J. Piedmont set up an office here (his specialty was land titles). And when it came time to consider the progress of our natal street, he could be counted on as an enthusiastic voice, seeking improvements in lighting, sanitation, and refuse collection.

But he was best remembered for his attempt to finally rid the community of plaguing canine hordes. For in those frontier times, which were the street's earliest days, dogs — just as presently — were known to trot about. Scores of mongrels, in fact. A traveler had to be alert not to stumble over a lazing pooch; dogs nipped at horses' legs (and in response, it was not uncommon for a rider to flash a pistol and shoot the animal on the spot); citizens complained that curs slept on sidewalks, pushed children down, tripped horse and rider, and filled the street with fleas. Aside from these worthy grievances, at night residents could barely sleep due to the inharmonious serenade of the unmusical beasts.

Our Elliot Piedmont considered these dogs to be a public nuisance of the highest priority.

So he raised funds for a roundup of the curs and offered local youngsters ten cents for every stray brought to a newly built pound.

All day long, as the story goes, the boys scurried through the street, lassoing the hounds with the riatas, and by late afternoon there was a remarkable scarce sighting of dogs, the only reminder of their existence being the chorus of howls and barks from the direction of the pound.

Elliot J. Piedmont was exceptionally pleased.

Except when some joker sneaked up the back way and opened the pound gate. Yelping hounds stampeded out the yard to freedom.

The next morning residents awoke to find the street overrun once more.

Elliot Piedmont declined the offer of the local boys, who were looking forward to another profitable day.

And he had to accustom himself to the poodles and wolfhounds and pups of mixed breed that continued to make the street their home.

The Unofficial History
Daniel

The street preacher, Daniel, stood at the corner of Piedmont and 5th, and began to shout:

Remember that Adam and Eve once lived in Paradise.

Oh, yes.

They did, they did.

In Eden they dwelled.

That's right! It's the truth I'm telling.

Where everything was touched by Him, molded by His hands. His presence in every blade, every dewdrop, every breath. All was perfect.

Until one day the devil, dressed in snakeskin, snuck in the garden, sidled himself up to Eve.

And how did Satan, except for his own dark

intellect, his cunning observation, know that of the two she was the one who was never content, that she had ambition?

And Eve went crazy for that snake, she went wild for him. There came a pride to her nakedness, a strange laugh in her throat, a change in the pace of her breath. But too bad for us, Mother Eve found out a delight in the unsacred and unholy.

And her innocence flapped its wings and flew away; it could not be captured again. The devil had a fine time too; for a while it became confusing who was schooling who. Still he kept his focus.

"Would you betray everybody for me?" he asked.

"Sure thing," she answered.

"Would you do wrong for me?"

"Yeah. Yeah," she promised.

And so the devil had corrupted Eve and she got on Adam and that is how we came to Piedmont Street. Yes, Neighbors; that is exactly how we arrived to this street.

Childhood
Cecile

He had the nerve to ask her (after the things they'd just done!) about her childhood. He'd stroked the curve of her jaw as he posed the question. In response, Cecile gave a derisive laugh.

And she remembered that,

Childhood was piano lessons.

It was Mother calling, "Cee-Cee. It's time to practice."

Miss White arriving at three o'clock.

Childhood meant the keys of the piano. It was playing do/re/mi/fa/so/la/ti/do. It was finger exercises.

It was a trio of blind mice and Are you sleeping, Brother John? The morning bells are ringing. Hear them ding, dong, ding! It was Twinkle, Twinkle, Little Star.

"Wonderful, Cecile! How well you are progressing!" and with black hands that resembled the wings of ravens, Miss White closed the music book.

Cecile's childhood was the braiding of hair.

It was tomato slices sprinkled with salt.

Her childhood was a spoonful of lemon and honey when she was sick with congestion in her chest.

(But it was not school, not yet. It was not ashes falling on Pompeii.)

Miss White rang the doorbell at exactly three o'clock. Her eyes had been crying. Why had her eyes been crying?

Childhood was a visit from Auntie.

It was not Lulu's hair on fire.

One day that would happen.

Lulu's hair ablaze on her head.

Childhood was not hair sparking, catching fire.

It was Mother serving slices of chocolate-frosting cake on pretty china plates.

It was Auntie wearing the moonstone brooch.

With an alert, displeased eye, Auntie watched Lulu (it was not Lulu's hair on fire!) gobble a third slice.

The smell, dark and delicious, of coffee percolating.

And Auntie was whispering that she heard the piano teacher was in a fix.

Now Mother sucked her teeth, shrugged a shoulder, and said in a low voice of her own, "Well, many a girl has got herself into big trouble. She's not the first, won't be the last either. Just the way of the world, I guess."

"The moral of this story is what every soon-to-be woman must learn," sighed Auntie. "Beware the Romeo, the I love 'em and leave 'ems. Watch out for the I'll call you in the morning, Honey-ers, the snakes in the garden, the sowers of seeds. — Lulu, daughter! You getting to be big as a house!"

Father had coins in his pocket, jingling a tune.

Childhood was summer and the Watermelon Man, driving by in his chip-painted truck. In lolling cadence he called out his rhyme.

Fine and Dandy
Tastes like Candy
Get 'em While You Can
Says the Watermelon Man.

Childhood was Father.

It was dear, sweet Father.

There was the chair where he sat when Cecile performed a parlor-room recital. Of course that was childhood too. Clap, clap, clap went his huge hands.

(Cecile remembers Miss White's hands, turning the sheets of music. Bare and dark, like the wings of a raven taking flight.)

Childhood was the taste of sour plums.

It was practice makes perfect and Pop! Goes the Weasel. And Sammy calling her name.

"All right," said Mother with a sigh. "All right."

Childhood was the swing in the shade of the trees. From the branches, red and purple blossoms dropped. Crows and ravens flapped their ebony wings.

How about a kiss? Sammy asked.

Hell! Cecile suddenly jumped up and began to dress wildly, already the blouse half-buttoned. I should never have kissed him. That was my downfall right there!

What's got you so upset, Darling!

Cecile was incensed. You had no right to, no right to put your nasty touch on...

What was once happy to me! What was innocence!

Rooster
Miz Prudehomme

The rooster is bronze colored, unremarkable in size. It has a candied, staring eye. The hens are white feathered.

"You trifling, no-good, son-of-a-gun. Go see to your women. Be a good husband," Miz Prudehomme chides. She means to sell the eggs, though she's never seen a farm in her life. She is from New Orleans, from Valence Street.

Unfortunately the egg business is not profitable. Instead Miz Prudehomme declares herself a beautician. She takes the hot comb from the stove burner, a red welt or two marking her forearm. Laughing, talking women visit her kitchen to get their hair straightened and styled. Meanwhile every Sunday a white chicken disappears. Last is the rooster.

She slits its throat with near-expert hands, for some matters are just so rooted in memory, so infinitely felt in flesh and marrow of bone. Though she's never been near a farm. She is from New Orleans, from Valence Street.

Fig Tree
Margaret

Many years ago the fig tree had been planted, now growing unpruned, spreading and generous. Rain. Sun. Soil. Rain. Sun. Soil. Every summer the figs ripen into purple pendants dangling on the branches.

And birds flock to a banquet.

Thieves! Scoundrels! Margaret shouts, roused to a rare fury.

Leaves shudder as the birds feast, gorging to their fill, splitting open the dusky husks, leaving behind half-eaten fruit; a bloody, pulpy, meaty mess with a thousand seeds, as she once imagined her own heart.

Garden

On her knees, she'd planted a garden of herbs and roots but understood nothing of their power and significance.

That dill, for instance, can protect oneself from the witchcraft of a rival.

How was she to know that? Or about lavender as a way to ease morning sickness? Or that now was the wrong time to plant a garden at all, she should wait until the phase of the full moon to sow her seeds.

Washing her hands in a dirty puddle, the woman stood and in the sky she saw the approach of another storm. For nearly a year there'd been extraordinary rains.

But drought was the season again with the pitiful leaves of the sprouts turned brown and desiccated, perfect for kindling.

Little Son

Here's the word on Little Son. He is a grown man with grey in his hair. He is maybe forty, fifty years old. Most men are GRANDFATHERS by that age.

He never has a woman. He has no job nor wants one. When the rains come and the roof leaks he does not worry, it's not his roof. Let the owner of the roof, the landlord or the landlady, put out a pot to catch the drops of silverlike mercury and a kettle to fill with sharp and flat notes of music. When the pot is hardened with sludge and minerals, when the kettle is discordant with a cacophony of noisy racket, the rain has been declared to CEASE AND DESIST.

―――――

And now Little Son is napping beneath a Tall Palm. He is passing the afternoon in a free and trackless drunken sleep with a dream so LUSCIOUS & sylvan & river-flowing & tamarind-plenty & milk 'n honeyed AND TROPICAL AND PRIMITIVE that it goes beyond dreaming, really, to reach into a vast and borderless memory, but which is still doomed to slip away from his grasp like ALL DELUSIONS, ALL REVERIES upon waking, like the vanishing tails of swimming away fish, like the extinguishments of comets.

Next, in the dream Little Son is playing a game of Dominoes at a picnic table with Adam, who was a happy fellow before his DISASTROUS FALL, and tells Adam to "Shuffle them bones." In his own hand is a Double Six and Jesus, dressed in lustrous white glittering with stars, is counting up the points.

Miz Prudehomme leans out her window, spots Little Son asleep under a Tall Palm and SPEAKING FOR ALL WOMANKIND fusses that he is a NO COUNT, LAZY, GOOD-FOR-NOTHING SHIFT-LESS UNWORTHY excuse for a man.

Her complaints and insults do not disturb his rest. Little Son goes on dreaming. All the while Jesus is tallying the points to declare a winner. The dream glides. JESUS IS DRESSED IN BLUE SKY RIBBONED WITH SUN RAYS. With a little stubby pencil, he is tallying the SCORE.

Meanwhile, the other two — including the one that is Little Son WHO YOU CAN'T COUNT ON FOR NOTHING, WHO IS ASLEEP UNDER A TALL PALM AS MR. CLARENCE LAYS THE PLUMBING FOR HIS STUCCO BUILDING ALL BY HISSELF ALTHOUGH LITTLE SON WAS SUPPOSED TO BE THERE AT NINE O'CLOCK SHARP TO HELP HIM AND MR. CLARENCE IS MUTTERING, "WHY DID I THINK THAT NO-GOOD ANY-EXCUSE-NOT-TO-DO-A-DAY'S-WORK SON-A-BITCH WOULD SHOW UP ANYWAY I SHOULD HAVE MY HEAD EXAMINED BUT HOW I WISH YES I REALLY WANT SOMETIMES TO BE HIM"; and the other that is ADAM WHO WAS A HAPPY BORN-LUCKY SOMEHOW-ALWAYS-MANAGES-TO-

GET-BY, WHY LET LIFE WORRY YOU?
PUZZLES THIS NOSTALGIC FIGURE OF A
LONG-AGO TIME, OH he was such an easygoing
NOTHING-DON'T-BOTHER-ME-MUCH mild-
mannered BROTHERMAN before his DISAS-
TROUS fall, saying CAN YOU GIVE ME A
DOLLAR? HOW ABOUT A CIGARETTE and A
LIGHT THEN? MUCHAS GRACIAS, SENOR: IN
OTHER WORDS, I APPRECIATE IT MISTER, the
two of them being a trifling pair — they are whistling
and kicking up their heels because in Little Son's mind
life is nothing but a good time.

Restaurant
Passerby

A passerby stopped in a small restaurant that stood on a corner. Inside were three men, including the one behind the counter. They were talking about the dogs that roamed Piedmont Street.

"A pack of 'em," said the big one. *"Mutts, mongrels, hounds —*Yesterday I counted thirteen."

"Thirteen — *bitches with teats swaying, flea-scratching, rabies-infected,"* said the one with glasses. "An unlucky number."

"I've run into 'em too," put in the counterman. "The leader with Terrier in him. They a menace, if you ask me."

"A health violation," the bespectacled one added.

"One day those dawgs — *trotting broken-legged*

down the center of a busy street, lapping from filthy gutters, knocking over trash cans for a bite to eat, whining and cowering — will chase a child down. You hear me? *AND TEAR HIM TO SHREDS,"* trumped Fatso.

The passerby ordered a sandwich and a glass of water. These he consumed mechanically, with an absent-minded, severe expression. He was handsome, almost. Yet there was something not quite right about him. His hair could use a trim and his face, despite the air conditioning, was sweating. The glass of water he drained promptly. Pointing, he called out, "I wouldn't mind more of this, if you can spare it."

The counterman brought the pitcher and poured, his eyes watching the Bible that had been placed on the counter next to a clean spoon. Once he finished pouring he went away.

And huddled with the other men at the opposite end of the counter. They were now different. The mood of the place was no longer easy and joking, talkative. The strange thing about this was usually strangers were welcomed here.

Daniel took another bite of cold ham. In short

time, he finished his sandwich and the second glass of water. When he left, there was enough money to cover the bill. And for that, the expression of the counterman relaxed in relief.

A Knock on the Door
Louise

We could tell it was him by the knock on the door. He would pound it, shaking the whole thing. Without mercy, without a flinch. Acting with the power and authority to break that door down. I stayed near the back of the kitchen, hands pressed on my knees, all ashy and tarred looking, peeked under the curtains of the breakfast-nook windows. "Ohdammit." And just because I saw Mama looking at me sideways through slit eyes I said it again. "Ohdammit. It's him." Everybody stayed still. Mama had been washing clothes in the sink on the back porch and suds crackled on her forearms. My sister Sheryl leaning against the doorway. We waited, but the knocking and pounding and trying to break the door down just wouldn't quit. And, after a while, Mama snatched a dishcloth from the rack above the sink, wiping her arms as she walked-ran to the door to let Uncle in.

From the kitchen I could hear the high-note girl-ish voice my mother uses for greeting company: Good morning, Brother. How you doing? He didn't say anything about the delay, but then he never did.

Sheryl and me rolling our eyes and scrunching our faces at each other. Her pulling frosted-polished fingertips through her bangs and dancing about eyebrows that had been nearly plucked gone. Sheryl's older than me by almost three years but has never seemed it. We stayed out of sight 'til we heard Mama calling: Girls, come in here and say hello to your Uncle.

He was sitting straight backed and alone on the couch, striped shadows across him caused by the sunlight filtering through the blinds. Arm draped awkward and stiff on the curled sofa arm, nothing but slipping plastic cover and empty-space stretched out beside him. Mama half-slumped in one of the green chairs, leaning her head against the blue sweater I had left hanging over the back. She had pulled the kerchief from her head and tugged at the ends with swollen, raw fingers.

I went up first, kissed our Uncle quick on his scratchy cheek. A chicken peck. He smelled different, sort of old, spoiling. While Sheryl took her turn I backed away, rushed to the only other chair in the living room. Didn't bother Sheryl none. She just strutted, that's the only word for it, over to Mama's chair, swinging her big butt, flashing the tip of her pink tongue at me, and perched real delicate-like on the arm. Made me wonder seriously why yellow-skinned, pretty-eyed Michael around the corner was always trying to talk to her instead of me.

The smell of cooking ham and black-eyed peas had trailed us into the living room, and I knew Mama and Sheryl were thinking the same as me, wishing we could pack up that smell, hide it 'til he was gone. I knew I didn't want my Sunday dinner spoiled by the sight of no-mannered him snatching at his food or hearing him fuss at Sheryl and me, telling us didn't we know better, you're supposed to stack the bread on a plate so a man doesn't have to always be asking for another piece.

No telling how long he would stay this time. I stretched out my arm, clicked on the TV, some silly early morning stuff, Popeye cartoons or something. Mama cutting her eyes at me; I turned down the sound. Just a little.

"How you been, Brother? Been a while since we've seen you. You looking good." Mama's fingers sliding down the clean slice that parted her hair, checking the bobby pins that locked her two braided knots in place. She had what the family called good hair; thick and straight, slightly flaring. But she always wore it up or covered.

I looked him over, decided that was a fib. He looked old and ragged; the dark suit he wore was frayed. Even so, Uncle Daniel still had a power to him, the only one of my dead father's brothers and sisters to come out with strong, distinct African features. He was a huge man, tall, with eye-drawing black skin deep and shiny as freshly polished patent leather. But his face was downcast, shaped by burden and gloom. And it was not likely to charm nobody.

In Uncle's large hands was cradled his Bible, a small

black one with *Holy Bible* etched in fancy gold letters. The Book had become so raggedy, the binding half torn off, and the pages soiled with fingerprints and dirt. We kept it our secret that in our family was a street preacher, one of those wild-looking men or women standing on Piedmont Street, in front of its downtown stores; one of those people lifting their arms to heaven and tumbling out words about sin and Sweet Blessed Jesus; one of those people others hurry past, hide their faces from. Yes, that was our Uncle.

"I'm doing just fine, Pearl. Praise God."

"Uh huh. Rose said you've been doing better. Said she got you to go to a clinic an—"

"That a lie! She tell you that? What a lie! That heifer ain't done a thing to help me. I wouldn't listen to her no how. Liar! She tried to poison me. I told you about that, didn't I? Yes, she did too. My own sister. She didn't tell you about that, now did she? But I tripped her up. Wouldn't eat nothin'. Just leave it there. On the plate. Every bite. You shoulda seen the act she put on then, Pearl. All that fussin' and wailin'. And the *cry-in*. Lord. Then the woman starts in again. On how maybe I should commit myself? Fiend. She-devil. Liar. I know what she's up to. Her and the rest. Hummph. Supposed to be my family."

Mama clamping her lips tight, rubbing her forehead and eyes with raw-edge fingertips, waiting for the thunderstorm to rage by. I could tell she was searching for something safe to say. "Well — "

"I wish B.J. was still here." Uncle stopped his haranguing and switched to a mournful tune. "If B.J. was still alive wouldn't none of this be happening." He rubbed his eyes, red-splashed eyes, and I wondered if maybe he'd started up drinking again. Mama and Aunt Rose mentioned how he used to drink a lot before taking up God.

I had been sneaking glances at the TV, looking down at my feet, which needed a washing. Looked anywhere but at him. Finally, I raised my eyes. He was staring right at me.

"How y'all doing in school?" he asked.

"Fine," I answered him, but turned my eyes back to the TV, tugged my fingers at the hem of my pink shorts. Every couple of minutes I would have to tear my thighs from the plastic seat cover, making a sucking, crackling noise.

"Oh, Louise's doing real good." Mama was resurrected. "That one gets nothing but A's." In my mind I'm rolling my eyes. I hated to be bragged on for my schoolwork. Next thing I knew Mama had jumped up and in three steps, all the while talking in her high company voice, was at the mantel over a fireplace we never used, her eyes reading over a jambalaya of family pictures, school awards, and knickknacks, arranged around a large, ornately framed picture of my father. Two fingers pinched together located and lifted the latest arrival, a third-place yellow ribbon I won in a school science fair, and she hurried over to gush to Uncle Daniel. I made some low noise, crossed my arms tight over my chest. Sheryl there twirling the ends of her hair, looking at something out the window. Made me wonder if Michael was passing by.

"Uh-huh." Uncle Daniel bobbing his head, grinning, leaning out of the striped shadows to look at the picture of Daddy. "Smart. Like him. He was smart too, growing up. Only one of us to make it. That's right.

Only one. Got to be a medical doctor. Just like he said. Yes sir. "The smile didn't change, and it did. I thought I knew why. Mama had told us. Him and Daddy never got along. Well, *he* never got along. She told us how Uncle Daniel would bust into Daddy's office full of patients or come here to the house, talking loud and ugly and threatening until Daddy gave him money or whatever else he wanted. She said how Daddy had to get him out of trouble all the time, out of jail or whatever. Everybody knew, Mama told us, things like that is what made Daddy sick so young. Now I don't remember any of these things, but Mama claimed them to be true.

He leaned back again into the zebra pattern. "I know you've had your troubles, Pearl. B.J. dying with the children so little and all. But the Lord must have had a reason. Yes sir. He must have had a divine plan."

Then it started. Lord this; Jesus that. The recitin' and chantin' and dronin' on about Repentance and Ignorant People and God's Fury. Lord have mercy. Lord have mercy. Lord have mercy on these stupid, common people who don't wanna know nothin'. I could feel a squeeze in my belly just waiting for him to open the

Bible and begin quoting Scripture. Mama was massaging her temples, nodding her head, mumbling every few moments, "We know it, Brother" or "Uh-huh, Brother." Sheryl shuffling her seat on the chair arm. Me — I could make his voice distant, look sideways at the TV or pick at a scab on my knee. But before long I felt something pricking at me. His voice. Something was wrong with it. I remembered it as a church-choir baritone, smooth and rich as melted chocolate. It sounded different, like he had to scrape the words from the sides of his throat, making them come out guttural and dead-sounding.

I looked at him again, closer. His eyes, once so black and strong and scary, were weak, barely standing out against a backdrop of watery red. His face was dragging; every move of his was heavy and slow, as if his body was underwater. But it was his voice that scared me most of all.

I saw him once.

(Listen to me.)

Preaching. I saw him preach once.

(I'm trying to tell ya.)

(I just come to tell ya.)

He didn't see me, I'm pretty sure.

(I'm almost through telling ya.)

I was waiting on the #54, going along Piedmont Street. I heard his voice first, felt a chill set in my face. Finally turning, seeing that it was him standing a little ways down the block. He was standing there, high on his toes, in front of what used to be a post office.

His voice was not tired then: *I tell ya one thing-ga. I tell you the truth, ha! (I try to bring you noos-sa. Not good news, no.) Although I tell you the tru-tha. Amen; Amen.*

Religion can't save ya now. No. Saying "Please Please" can't help ya now. No. Time's past for begging; Time's past for mercy. (Though He pities you. I pity you.) Too late for your false promises to LooktaGodLooktaGodLooktaGod.

Different than his living-room sermons. It was music: a sorrowful alto rocking, holding. Words coming out. Stop and go. Words spit out, spilling out: kissed words; hushed words, swelling; shouted words screamed in a raspy voice. One hand gripping that familiar Bible. Arms swinging, pointing, lifting. Body jerking. Toes

138

tapping. All to the melody of his chants. What is he doing? Face earnest and strained.

(What I come to tell ya, what He told me to tell ya.)
Amen; Amen. Amen; Amen. Only it's the tru-tha I tell ya, and it's not good. But it's the tru-tha, and I'm almost through telling ya. Yes, I'm almost through.

(Listen to me. Listen to me. Listen to me, y'all.)

Squeezing myself on the green wooden bench, peeking over a mean-looking lady sitting next to me to watch him, never looking too long, too scared that my staring would draw his eyes to mine. Ducking behind the mean lady every time he turned my way. Did he see me?

Still, I could not keep myself from watching. People trotting past him, stepping out of their paths, away from him. They kept their heads down.

I tell ya thisss-sa. I tell you the tru-tha.

People trotting by.

I tell ya. I'm just telling ya. Amen; Amen.

Him stretching out that big hand, reaching out but holding back, too. After a while his face grew twisted, ugly. "Sinners," he spat. Then wailed. "Sinners. Sinners."

What must have shown on my face if anyone in the bus-stop crowd had bothered to look at me.

The bus was coming. Through the unfolded accordion doors I escaped and found a seat next to a grinning man, and made myself not look back.

Uncle Daniel stopped his sermon. His face and withered chicken neck were all wet and he reached two fingers into his breast pocket, drawing out a cloth handkerchief, clean and white. Draping the cloth across his large palm he brought his perspiring black face down, smothered it in the starched whiteness and rubbed.

"How y'all enjoying your Sunday?" Crumpling the handkerchief now. Blowing his nose with rude, loud snorts.

We all got real quiet. I remember thinking: Jesus, please don't let him ask to stay for dinner. Please, God. And even though it was a silent prayer I made sure not to look at Uncle.

When he spoke his voice squeezed out low and small, and he bobbed his head softly. "Smells good."

Mama nodding her head, too, at nothing really, and Sheryl tugging, tugging at her bangs.

"I had wanted to take y'all out. But, well, my checks haven't come yet. Nice place too, Pearl. Good cooking."

"Oh, that's all right, Brother. You don't have to be spending your money on us anyhow. You have little enou—"

"I know I don't have to. I didn't say I had to." Something in his voice made us all silent, hateful.

He got quiet too, just sat there, waiting, his thumb stroking the Bible. After a few moments, "Could ...somebody...get...me...a...glass...of...water? PLEASE." Uncle Daniel asked in a way that made Sheryl and me stop sneaking silly looks and jerk our heads to face him with startled eyes. Sheryl was quicker than me that time, leaping up and leaving me there.

We could hear pot covers rattling and clanging; Sheryl taking her time, checking the dinner, probably lowering or cutting off the cooking fires. Mama talking to him in her high-pitched voice, but I'm not listening to the words. What is wrong with him, I was thinking, to make us so mean?

About this time Uncle erupted — a fit of quaking coughs that shook Mama and me, too, made us snap our eyes to him, scared. Mama called to Sheryl (and now her true voice came back, the one I knew) to Hurry UP With That Water Now, and she rushed to the kitchen with pounding steps. The moment Mama left he settled down again. Almost quiet now, just his chest heaving. And then I realized we were alone. I folded my arms and crossed my legs, tried to make myself small; turned my eyes away but saw him there just the same. When I looked at him, finally, he was watching me.

"Does it hurt?" I wanted to know, and his watery eyes studied me.

"Sometimes," he answered. "Always when I least expect. Sometimes it waits. Pain. And comes later. Keeps me from getting a full night's sleep." A few more coughs came; ugly and scraping. When they were finished he tried to smile. "You know what? You look just like your Daddy. Ha. Just the image. Guess you hear that enough, huh?"

He was leaning forward, watching me, lips holding

on to the smile. But I'm not ready to give anything. Uncle Daniel fell back, his black bony fingers spread wide over his knees.

Mama and Sheryl now back, standing there I don't know how long; Sheryl holding a long, pink glass of water. Uncle standing, taking the glass. Him stretching to his full, massive height, leaning back his head, tilting the glass, drinking the water in three noisy swallows. Three tight knots I could almost see traveling down his throat.

He hugged his Bible to his chest. "Y'all enjoy your dinner now," he said. "I was just paying a visit." He waited at the door, briefly. And then he was gone. All of us — Mama, Sheryl, and me — standing there; must have been just a minute. We listened to him leave. The slam of the door and the peace that followed it.

Train

It's plain bad luck to have to wait for a train. It moves along like a mammoth herd crossing. Freight car after freight car, never-ending. And no choice but to be patient. Its lackluster roar sustained with equilibrium in our ears.

❖

It's worse luck however to come across a funeral procession. In broad day a black-headed serpent, eyes white and glaring. Miles and miles it slinks along the avenue. On its way, on its last journey.

❖

That morning she'd been worried that she'd forgotten to cut the fires of the stove off.

If she turned back to check, she'd be late for her appointment.

But if she kept going, then there'd be the dread of returning home to nothing but devastation.

❖

When
It Burned to the Ground

I

Arriving to the day when the sky crowned itself with a dazzling nimbus that could be mistaken for a second dawn.

From the coils of black smoke you could tell what burned. The grocery. The corner liquor store. The meat market...

All Piedmont Street ignited.

When it burned to the ground.

There was the smell of tar, but it lingered from a roof repair and was not the blacktop melting beneath our feet.

II

When Miz Prudehomme saw that the Piedmont Street emporium was on fire she sucked her teeth. Not a grain of sugar was left in the house. Now there'd be none for the morning's coffee, which would be bitterly swallowed down her throat.

III

The emporium was also where she shopped for butter and cream, okra, onions, as well as three lbs. of rice; it was where she went when she happened to need a bar of soap, a nice little cake, and camphor to keep moths from the closet.

IV

I heard the cries of pandemonium: shouts and bellows, and the howl of an old woman.

Eve's Daughter
Bernadette

1) Long ago there were two trees.

They, the original ones, reached the first tree and ate its fruit. Well, that caused misery. Yet they did not get to the harvest of the other. Maybe that was for the best. Probably it would've only caused misery too.

These words that I remember now, in this hour, were not mine; they were said by my mother. But she was a pained, sad woman who courted death. Widowed young, a seamstress who had to work too hard to make the few dollars that kept her in a state of worry, for her this life promised no paradise. I rarely saw my mother smile (probably little enough was offered for her to find amusing) but the few times she did feel a bit of gladness she hid her quiet laugh behind the cover of a corded, blanched hand. What else? — That she was a thin woman (willowy and graceful in her relative youth, gaunt by the time of middle age) and love is not what I think of when remembering her as much as pity.

When I felt this pity I was very small, not in school even. But I was not a usual child. That nightly ceremony bidding us to kneel beside our tiny beds, the terrible prayer all other children scrambled through without thought or understanding, those very words "and if I should die," declaring outright I might never wake again. No, I wouldn't ever say them. Already I was aware of death.

So this was my childhood. A tiny room where the dressmaking dummy stood in the corner and an old table covered with baskets of thread and lace and buttons. Mother sat in a wooden chair, a piece of fabric, gabardine or linen, in her hands, her fingers hurrying to baste a cuff to a sleeve or slipstitch a hem.

Her eyes kept on her work, but she felt I was nearby. So when she began to speak it was not to herself, as it may have seemed, but to me. She spoke urgently, pressingly, and always of heaven. It was her sole topic. And what a glorious lush portrait of Shangri-La she painted so richly with scarlet and gold and king's purple, before she would add, "This world is not meant to last, of course. Its sufferings are impermanent. This world is a mere watermark. To leave here means to journey to a better one populated by souls. That's where I'll soon be. And I'll be happy there."

All this talk of death. I became as used to it as the whistles and songs of the birds in the sky. How many times I heard these words and the next.

"Be glad for me when I go. As for yourself, don't love it here too much, Bernadette. That is no good.

"Because trouble comes to those who do. It's why I say, be careful, Daughter. People can bring hardship onto themselves."

Out the back window was a view of our yard. And to me it was as beautiful as Mother's promised Eden. Roses grew there and honeysuckle. Also a bird of paradise, prospering after a season of rains. The bush was dazzling with flaring blossoms, flowers with a brightness that seemed forever burning. As my stare stayed on it, I felt wonder. And in that moment I understood only those who cling to their lives here.

In the yard was also an orange tree, a startling burst of color against a bland blue sky. It had grown huge and spreading and at times burdened with fruit. When I was eleven or twelve, my mother told me to pick as many oranges as I could and to sort them carefully. Some of the others we would keep for ourselves, and the rest I should bring to a neighbor who lived across the street.

When the neighbor opened his front door, I saw that he still wore the green uniform with the name of the company he worked for embroidered on a patch near his shoulder. He opened the door wider; I stepped across the shiny tin threshold.

The neighbor was a bachelor and he seemed to have adjusted to that lot as his destiny. The room we stood in was dusted, the floor swept. Bright clean curtains decorated the windows and in the air was the roasting aroma of his dinner. (Flavored with sage; by heart I knew that herb's fragrance.) It was my first visit to the neighbor's house, though he himself was familiar enough to me.

Yet I thought he looked at me strangely as I handed him the bowl of oranges. I said, "They're very sweet. Mother said to bring them to you."

He waited before taking the bowl. Then he asked, and I should say here that this neighbor had a particular voice. It was weary and battered as if it must have had a dragged and difficult passage through his throat; and so in that awful voice he asked what from any other speaker might have been a polite and sociable question, "How is your mother?"

"Not well," I replied.

"I am sorry to hear that," he answered seriously.

And now his voice, made strong with a certainty, made his next words seem the only and very frightening truth, "A good, decent woman — modest and sacrificing as your mother," he said, "— is a rare thing. Most others of that persuasion ain't nothing but deceivers. You can't trust 'em. You can't do enough for 'em. Men fall to their sex, whimper and do wrong and run up debts. Oh, bad women! They think it's fun to ruin a man, to cause him suffering. Yes, yes. That type is a far more common breed.

"Ah, but even those wenches don't compare to you in wickedness."

Before these words, this neighbor had never before seemed anything but indifferent toward me, so they were the only warning to what happened next. He let go the bowl of oranges, all of which dropped to the rug-covered floor with a dull bouncing racket. His hands snatched my shoulders, held me in a clutch. And he brought his face down close to mine. "I been keeping a watch on you, Bernadette." Until that moment, I would never have even thought he could call me by name. "I know just what you are. When you played with the other children, shouting and tearing up and down the block, I spotted you. The others here don't know yet. Just me. Just me. I see you. You not really one of us. You never mean to be happy with what we have. But we'll be the ones to suffer for your misdeeds.

"And now I want you to answer me, why you been

stealing my hairs? Don't lie to me either! Last night I woke just in time to catch sight of you. You plucked the hair right out of my head." He reached up to touch a balding patch. Such a mild-looking, ordinary man he seemed. His eyes were dull and brown. Only now, standing so close, did I see the crazy in them.

Something on the stove — a pot of rice, I think — began to scorch. While in that beleaguered voice, the neighbor went on. "What evil you mean to do to me, huh? You want to hurt me because I recognize you for what you are? Well, what if I don't give you the chance?"

His lips smiled and his cheeks dimpled. He said, "Don't you know I met your kind once before? The worst of females, she too meant to bring Wrath on us all. Yes, yes. She tried to defy the way things supposed to be.

"But I took care of her; I did. Uh huh. I found out it was fire she feared. How her nappy plaits ignited like the wicks of candles. How she screamed and coughed and twitched and pumped them stockinged legs. And a bitty hill of ashes was all that was left.

"Huh, that's right. That's what I did to finish off her."

I began to cry, wrenchingly, I was so frightened. Though at first he said the tears were trickery, I suppose he eventually took a look at the sobbing young girl standing before him and came to his senses. His face became worried, and he lost his bluster, saying:

"No, no. You can stop that hollering. That was a long time ago. I'm not looking for no trouble today, eh, eh, eh. Don't need no police coming here, no thanks. I'm done with that. All I want is to live my life quiet. Keep myself to myself. The world don't need me as caretaker. It can fend for itself.

"Thank you for the oranges, Bernadette. Remember now, I didn't do you no harm. So you go on home now."

❖

I did go home. Mother was working at the sewing machine, she and apparatus making a half-and-half creature that spun out yards of sugary crinoline. Her foot lifted off the pedal in hovering pause. "So you took the oranges to Mr. _____," she made distracted comment. Then the foot bore down again. The machine's noisy working overcame any answer I could have given, and, concentrating on a stitch, she didn't turn to catch glimpse of my face.

As for that neighbor, from time to time I saw him, most often as he was leaving for his job or returning home with a paper sack of groceries cradled in the crook of his arm. One day Mother and I spotted him standing in his yard across the street, holding what looked like a fitful conversation with no one but hisself. "Poor man is having a nervous breakdown," observed Mother. "Poor, poor friendless man."

2) I was nineteen when death at last came to my mother, but it was not as easy and kind as she thought it would be. It was not as lovely.

And I saw for myself what had been her lies, her tales, for I was witness to it all. I saw death rollick in her. I saw death and of course I feared it.

(Bernadette, why do you despise death; why do you quarrel with it so? people ask. In answer I point to this day, my mother's passing, and in my measuring view its cruelty, its merciless triumph over the weak and defenseless.)

Already the white nightgown she wore, as if a bride, was soiled, ragged, the ribbon ripped away. And soon enough her eyes were wide with truly seeing.

Perhaps Death asked her, for somebody seemed to be whispering in her ear, *Don't you welcome me, your old friend, at all?*

"No," I heard her murmur. "No. No. No."

Ah, but it is too late to change your mind now, Dear.

She cried out, "I see a fiend. With a mark on his lip. Bernadette has such a stain. When people asked I told them that as a baby she had fallen, that it was a scar. But the truth is Bernadette was born with that mark."

Soon she begged for the doctor's medicine and finding its prescription useless she cursed, cursed life and death as if they were the same, a sly-grinned hunchbacked old man who stood at the foot of the bed. With chapped lips she spat out cuss words I had no idea she knew much less could fling out so shame-lessly.

Oh, I would have liked to run, to have left that house and stayed away from it all, to hide myself in the dusk. Out the window was the bird of paradise, but it was November and it had no flowers, no candlelit blossoms to light the darkness soon to come. For in a matter of an hour night was coming for us all, and the orange tree and all the garden would be a memory even for the living.

Eventually my mother spent her curses, but there was not silence. She now struggled for air, and for quite a while I watched the exaggerated rise and fall of her chest. Therefore breathing was her instinct too, I thought as I listened to that jarring music. Never had I felt more tenderness for her or the deepest, purest pity. Never had I felt more kinship.

That was when I reached for my mother's hand, already cold. I kept gentle hold of it as dark like a vapor eased into the room.

"Should we say one of your prayers?" I asked. She nodded.

Except for her slurred speech, she sounded like herself again, repeating her devotions, her Hail Marys and Our Fathers, until the final effort. Until the last desire of the body to breathe.

A new moon hung unseen in the sky when I folded my mother's arms across her chest in that ancient repose. I pulled up the sheet but could not cover her face. So I drew the sheet as far as her shoulders. As if the dewy night might chill her, I tucked her in her bed.

She looked merely asleep, and I remembered myself as a child, how each night her slumber seemed like death. Yet in the morning she woke. Such relief I felt. Such reprieve. Now, just as when I was seven, I sat nearby her bed and watched for her to wake. But after an hour or two, I knew; I knew.

My mother was dead.

Immediately there were matters of business to conduct. I was the one to arrange a funeral, as simple and modest as her life. There, proper speeches befitting a good Creole widow were spoken, and these were words I knew would never be said about me. Among a small gathering under the noon sun I listened as the priest said of my mother, "She is home. And never have I seen any member of this parish who so understood the meaning of this, the magnificence. What an example for those of us who are hesitant, hoping that this day will not come. Such a day does arrive. And this fine woman for so long yearned to return to our Lord's Paradise. Her fervent desire being to flee this imperfect world. And to reside once more in that holiest of cities.

"Oh, that this dear humble woman held the knowledge the more learned, the pedantic, the book-fed do not. She grasped the profundity, and in her honor, I will remind you. Our lives here are in passing. Our time is intended to be short. We should, like her, hold little allegiance to this place."

My thoughts were vicious.

But my face must not have shown them. When, afterwards, the priest approached me, his expression remained kind and sympathetic. I shook his hand. And what a heavy, huge hand it was, this disrespectful thought was in my mind, more suited to a bricklayer than a holy reverend. I had that thought again as he lay that massive slab on my head for a blessing, the last I would ever receive.

I had already seen to it that she would be buried next to my father. Sorrow I felt, yes, at their loss, but also the lightheartedness of release.

To be done with dying! To be done with it!

And now to live. Because that, I'd made my decision with headstrong boldness, was what I'd set myself on doing.

3) The next day I put on a dress printed with pink hibiscus to meet with the landlord, Mr. Perriliat, whose taut, unchanging features I had seen all my life, every first of the month when he came to collect the rent.

I wonder if he still lives. Is that possible? People talked about him too, though not as much. He was fair-skinned and from some foreign, quite different place. When his brother came along Mr. Perriliat could be heard to speak a language we could never figure out. He had money and traveled to collect rent in cars only a rich man could afford, the latest parked at the curb being a Cadillac, itself dollar-green, its polish reflecting our entranced stares. Of course there nurtured in us ill will and envy. Though to his face people said, "How you doing, Mr. Perriliat? How is your honey-voiced, pretty wife?" and smiled, but as soon as he drove off there were mutters and peculiar comments that must have raised my curiosity because once I asked him:

"Are you as old as the earth?"

"Nearly as old, girl. Nearly as old."

"And you took a drink from the fountain of youth?"

"Oh, I've drunk from many a well and spring and fountain. That's for sure."

"Are you, because this is what they all keep saying, the richest man there is?"

"If I was, I would not mind it."

"But is it true you can buy anything with money?"

"I say it's worth a try, girl. It's worth a try."

Returning to this hour, the day following my mother's funeral. Mr. Perriliat's inspection of the house (an easy labyrinth of a few, narrow rooms) revealed to him all he needed to know, that I had scrubbed the floor clean to its corners, that the fixtures were not stolen, that the rugs were beaten free of all dust.

Satisfied, he said, "I'm truly sorry to lose such fine tenants. You been the best of them, that's for damn sure. I tell you it is a hard thing to be a landlord these days. Oh, trust me, my life is nothing but hardship. Between the city's red tape and the caliber of tenants, it's no wonder my blood pressure is so high. People should have more pity for the landlord. Though I have not encountered much understanding myself."

Glints of grey, I noticed, were coming into Mr. Perriliat's brow; otherwise, there was no sense of time to his face, which was unbothered.

"And you can bet with my bad luck the next occupants of this house will be every time late with the rent or one night doze off with a cigarette burning and the place will go up in flames. It's a shame how people do."

His gaze had settled on my packed things, which included my mother's sewing machine, because I planned to be a seamstress too.

When he looked my way, his shoulders shivered.

"Was it always so drafty in here?"

"Yes, Mr. Perriliat."

"Probably then the new tenants will complain about that too. Well, I'll just say to you good luck, Miss Bernadette. Good luck to you."

Yes, good luck to me! Already I had my coat on. It was made of a light cloth, just warm enough for the low wind that blew as I stepped out the door.

One last thing, the neighbor across the street, the one I brought oranges to that time. He was at his picture window, watching as I left. And while the driver was packing the trunk of the cab with my belongings, I waved boldly to him.

My neighbor let go the curtain then, but before it hid him from view, I saw. His head, by now, was bald.

4) I came to Piedmont Street, which then was modestly prosperous. There was a bread factory that kept people working, and although miles away the smell of a thousand baking loaves reached me, a smell I found both marvelous and sickening. There were

middle-class stores, a bank, a post office, and what the people now call The Old Theater was at that time a popular movie house. The street itself was trafficked and brisk.

So this is the world, I thought, and of course a person must make her living.

I looked for employment and found it in a seamstress shop owned by a Miz LaSalle. But she did not have me sorting threadspools by color or toting bolts of material for long, as it turned out I had a talent for dressmaking far better than my mother and beyond the rival of Miz LaSalle herself.

Can it be possible there is artistry in a trade like this? That the point of a collar can be a masterpiece? That there is joy and pride in a pocket? And genius in the choice of a button? Can there be conceit in a zigzag stitch? Or renown in arranging a skirt to drape an ample hip flatteringly?

How can it be, when both use the same pattern, that a dress made by one differs so remarkably from that sewed by another?

"Bernadette has a talent for this," mentioned Miz

shine, read a glamour magazine or a few chapters of a book. Sometimes I sang along with the radio. And when I had appetite, I ate, a hot bowl of grits with butter and salt, a slice of toast and apple butter.

Tuesday at ten o'clock I went back to work. Usually, Miz LaSalle had arrived already and unlocked the door. If she was late I waited on the step until she came up, bearing no apologies.

A day did come when something out of the commonplace happened. A young woman walked into the shop. She was the same age as I but all our lives we had lived in different sections of the city. It was simply fact that in different hospitals we were born (and it would not surprise me if it was on the same day), in different schools we learned our childhood lessons, and in different cemeteries our own were buried so that they could lie in familiar and comfortable company. This was the way things were and because of that we should have kept on without a meeting between the two of us. Yet here she was in Miz LaSalle's shop, and she looked very much the timid, nervous stranger in a distant land.

When she came into the shop I was busy at the sewing machine, the thrumming pump of the needle numbing my ears, so I did not hear her cross the threshold or ask for me by name. I did not hear Miz LaSalle's parrot calling out *Goo Morning! Goo Morning!* I did not hear Miz LaSalle's annoyed shout. I did not hear my employer's tiny sharp steps coming at me. I did, however, feel the push on my shoulder. That was when I turned and first saw the young woman.

— What is it you want here?

— A dress, she said. A very special dress for a once-in-a-lifetime occasion.

— Aren't there seamstresses on your side of town?

— Of course, she answered. But I want to come to you.

— And why would that be?

— Because you, Bernadette, have developed a far-reaching reputation. People are saying that you are the almost-unheard-of-rarity. You are a descendant of

Cinderella's godmother, a miracle worker, a heaven-kissed and magical couturier. They say that you can turn even an ugly woman like me into a beauty.

— It'll cost you a fortune.

— Yes, infringed Miz LaSalle, the best does cost money.

— Fine, the stranger said, with not even a moment to consider or to try to barter. She said it again, Fine.

When it was time to leave and I had put on my jacket, Miz LaSalle called: "Bernadette, I have a surprise for you. Listen." In a few short hours she had taught her green parrot to say, *In LaSalle's shop, miracles are performed. In LaSalle's shop, miracles are performed. In LaSalle's shop, miracles are performed.*

6) Of course I was not meant to stay an apprentice for very long. I had ambition though I kept it my secret. All my planning was in my head, all the saving I did was managed discreetly, all the extra work I took on was done furtively. Yet perhaps Miz LaSalle knew. She offered me two and a half times my pay.

Thank you, I said. Still my mind was set.

The day came when I gathered my sewing basket and walked out the door to my own store, just two blocks away.

And I tell you only the most stubborn and misery-loving customers stayed with her. Even Miz Washington came with me, although she had been a patron of Miz LaSalle for some twenty years.

7) From the start I had more than enough clients. So when a year later the bell above the door thumped its little metal heart I actually dreaded the arrival of a new order (because everybody needed something special, astounding; everybody wanted it quickly). That day especially I was nearly falling asleep. For almost a month I had opened the shop early and worked through my lunch and dinner hours. But I knew I was too greedy to send away a customer. Still, it was with cranky resentment I thought to myself, "What will it be this time — a confirmation dress, a debutante gown?"

When I looked up from my task (I had, with the pull of a thread, been gathering the puffed sleeve of a spoiled girl's party dress), there in the doorway stood Miz LaSalle.

"It's nice of you to come for a visit," I said.

"A visit," she replied. All her bitterness toward me showed itself in her tone. "You call it a visit."

"Well, if it's not a visit, I won't offer you tea with some whiskey in it, like I know you like. And if this isn't meant to be a happy little get-together, Miz LaSalle, what brings you here?"

"A meeting!" She took pleasure in announcing. "A meeting between us that's been overdue. Besides," she went on, "I came to see what a successful shop looks like."

As she spoke, she began a strolling tour of the front room, and soon came upon a rack of orders already completed and hung. When she touched one particular sleeve I made comment, "See the stitching on that cuff? —You can't find that everywhere."

"Yes, very beautiful," she agreed, "but you've always had an unexplainable touch."

Then her gaze settled on an outfit in an unusual

shade of blue. "How is my old friend, Miz Washington?" she asked. "I haven't seen her in ages."

"She ordered three of those suits," I answered.

"And yet," Miz LaSalle continued, turning to look at me, "she was the first to warn me about you, Bernadette."

I believe I sighed, finishing the sleeve and beginning immediately on the other; my actions showing what I meant them to: there was too much work waiting to have my time wasted.

Miz LaSalle was frowning as she watched. Still frowning, she asked, "What is it like to have everything go your way? To have nothing but good luck? Because my luck, you see, has not been so good. The thing is I've been having all sorts of trouble. My beloved parrot, which has always kept me company, flew away. I've had a toothache for the past two weeks. And worst of all I argued most viciously with Mr. LaSalle, during which he said things that cannot be absolved. Beyond indecent, the impulses he admitted to. I'll never again sleep soundly next to the man.

"It is amazing how everything has turned for me.

It seems ever since you've come to this street, Bernadette, I've had bad fortune."

"You sure enough thought me good fortune in the beginning," I reminded her with some bitterness of my own. "Four bridesmaid gowns not done with the wedding in a week and the bride-to-be throwing a fit, prepared to slander you at the least, and more likely to blacken both your eyes if I hadn't worked without two nights' proper sleep to help you finish in time."

For what felt like a long while Miz LaSalle looked at me. "Bernadette, there's something not right about you!" she said, suddenly fierce, no longer restrained. That's when I noticed that her hair was uncoifed and grey at its roots, her mouth without lipstick was unremarkable bare flesh. Small, amiss details but how little anarchy it took to make her resemble a madwoman. So what I had heard, though I of all people put little regard to gossip, was undoubtedly true. The last of her patrons had deserted her and soon more than likely would be bringing their business to me.

Her eyes saw that I knew and so she admitted,

though speaking the words sprung tears in her eyes. "My shop is closing. LaSalle's shop is closing."

"I'm sorry to hear."

"Oh, don't even say it, don't lie, you nasty thing." Tears welled again and she worked her hands in a busy yet purposeless manner. "I even went to see a woman. People said she could help me."

Now I must have looked at her funny because Miz LaSalle turned her head. She was that ashamed, yet she went on with pitiful muster.

"She lived in a yellow house at the other end of Piedmont Street. She's lived there for thirty years, but I'd never heard of her. It was others who knew her. I stay away from devil's work. It's devil's work.

"But how else to fight you, Bernadette? How else to stop such an enemy?

"So I traveled to her little yellow house up there in the hills. I would recognize it, I was told. A giant fig tree would be the landmark and a garden of hyacinth.

"I had to hold my handkerchief to my nose. The tree's rotting fruit had a rich, too sweet smell that was sickening. As I passed the garden I saw it was choked with weeds. The house needed painting, the porch step that was my greeting broke beneath my foot. What kind of common people have I got myself mixed up with? I thought. Almost I turned around. But the grown daughter came to the door and took my money and it was too late.

"The daughter led me to the kitchen where a woman in a gingham apron was shelling peas. She nodded at me and grinned, but did not have the manners to offer me a seat. So I stayed standing in the middle of the floor.

"The old woman kept shelling peas as she talked. Oh, how she talked. Such mighty brave words. She'd lay you low, she said. She'd make you wish you'd never come to this street. She had heard of you. I was not the first to mention you, oh no. You are known, Bernadette.

"What hope that granny gave me! I kissed the hands perfumed with green peas because they would work against you. I kissed her yellow cheek. My shop would be saved.

"But she couldn't help. She was nothing but a thief. Or, Bernadette, she was just not as strong as you."

"What nonsense, Miz LaSalle!" I said calmly, heartlessly.

"Maybe," she answered, her face unconvinced. But I insisted, "Of course it's nonsense. Of course it is."

Because I worked hard and without holidays, in short time I bought a house in an enclave off Piedmont Street. I had a Spanish-tile roof and a wonderful stained-glass picture window, the only one in the neighborhood.

There I lived by myself. I had no mother, no father, no grandparents. I had no aunts or cousins. I had no children. I felt that I was always to be solitary, to remain private; I was to belong solely to myself.

8) I am not an ungrateful person. No one can ever say that of me. So I was grateful for Tom Summers, for the first sight of him jaywalking across the street. I was grateful for this time of happiness and grateful still after it was gone.

Why should I tell about this, then, what was long ago and brief in its lasting (and so I must be brief in the telling), except to show that even my life would know love, that I would love and be loved, and no matter how many years have passed since, no matter how quickly it was to vanish, such a happening is unforgettable; still it remains the most important thing.

That day Tom Summers appeared in my life, the exact moment, because I remember it, was a rare one, without busyness in a life of industry. I sat idle at my worktable littered with scraps of fabric, the machines had been recently oiled, and that heavy, clogging odor dominated the air.

At my elbow was a bowl of fruit, spilling over with apricots and plums, dates and tangerines. And as I nibbled I watched Piedmont Street through the window. I watched Tom Summers make his reckless jaunt through traffic and I watched him head directly to my shop's door.

So this is love, I learned at the age of thirty-nine. So this is joy: it wore a suit and a hat.

My Tom wore a suit and a hat. The hat with a red feather in its band was too old for him. Now about the suit, well that it was bought at discount from a dead man's family did not amaze me. Certainly no tailor had ever measured him for it. The sleeves were ill-fitting, too short, and from an abrupt, ludicrous end poked out a golden brown hand that curled around the handle of a battered briefcase which he set on the floor as if he'd already been invited to stay.

"What have you come to sell me?" I asked immediately.

Tom's eyes seemed impressed. "So you are a businesswoman not to be trifled with, I can see that. Fine, since you've brought it up so quick — I guess you don't waste your time with small talk, although I don't mind a little conversation myself. Certain people can be interesting to get to know. But so many of 'em is in a rush these days. They don't have the patience no more. So I'll get right to it — "

"Then get to it," I said in a rough tone. Still we both grinned.

"All right, then. All right. I come to see you about what you might think money cannot buy. And that is tranquility — a bit of tranquility from the worried state of being that is our undisputed legacy."

"Is that right?"

"Oh, I'm certain a sensible-minded, conscientious tradeswoman like yourself knows that disaster may strike at any moment. Floods, earthquakes, high gusts of wind. What if this very fine auspicious shop burns down? Huh?"

"So let it burn down. A shop can be rebuilt," I countered.

Tom Summers leaned in. Broad and handsome his face was, majestic and slow-moving as a mountain. He said, "But where'd be my commission in that?"

He was vain to the point of being a peacock. He bought the suit not just because it was a bargain but because he felt he looked sharp and professional wearing it. He was not so honest, as the next conversation shows.

Because eventually I would come to ask him, recalling the day we met, if you loved me at once as you say you did, then why did you also try to cheat me?

"Don't deny it now," I said. "The fact is I caught you adding the same figure three times."

"I won't deny either one, that I loved you and

would've taken slight advantage of you too. But that's business, Honey. It's the way of the world."

"True," I admitted. "To get by you must have some tricks up your sleeves. You must have some ruthlessness."

Tom Summers was a man. Tom Summers was soon to become my husband. Across the busy trafficked street he crossed to reach me. That was the day love came into my life. For a short while, it stayed.

Morning came. And what comes with morning? Not the early dawn with its formless light but morning in its brashness, showing all. With morning was my black hair in loose waves with Tom's fingers tangled in the strands. With morning was his easygoing grin. With morning he rolled toward me and I was faced with the blue-ink scrawl "Player" engraved above his heart.

❖

"You'd think she'd know better. But word is Bernadette's gone crazy over Tom Summers."

In my shop, women waited their turns to be fitted.

They whispered — or neglected to — as I listened on the other side of a heavy drape, finishing up alterations for Miz Arceneaux.

"I thought something was different about her," said another. "She's looking too good. Barely a day over eighteen, if that."

"Well, happiness, laughter, affection are good for the looks," offered a third. "Dancing close, lovemaking, kisses are the best medicinals for one's constitution."

"How'd she get a man so much younger? He can't be more than twenty-five."

"Oh, I hear he just made twenty."

"Can that be right?"

"His Mama was there the day he was born. And she's pretty adamant. Now to me, and mind you I'm a few years younger than Bernadette, that is nothing but a little baby."

"A baby, I'll say! Always thirsty for a tit to suckle!"

Without a doubt this was meant to remind me.

Of the one who worked at the market. She trembled as she handed me my change.

And also there were the twins who did not look alike. One bought Tom a medallion to wear around his neck; the other a watch he checked to see when he was running late.

Yet only one woman concerned me and with good reason stoked my jealousy. Her name was Adrienne and she and I would never meet. I heard she was young, with a heart-shaped face perfectly carved of polished cherrywood: the small mouth and the little bumps of cheeks, the fine brow and nose. Such a remarkable face, as described to me, must have taken delight in itself, a pardonable and natural pride.

"Just so strange," continued the women in my shop as I, in the private room, meticulously and without hurry attended to Miz Arceneaux. She was elderly and stout and deaf. So in a customary unawares she stood, my chalk markings of alterations etched on her unfinished dress; slightly she swayed in a far away world, all of her own particular making, and from any ugly intrusion she was undisturbed, she was protected. Her iron-grey head slightly cocked, her aged face dumb and mild, she did not hear them say, "Just strange that a girl young and healthy should all of a sudden start losing her teeth. Every tooth in her mouth, not a single one remaining."

A shame, I admitted to myself.

❖

And what about the night? What comes with night, which has its own creatures? What shows itself only in the dark? When Tom was through kissing me, when he was exhausted and weak and held in my arms, sometimes a vise, then were his fears and accusations. His harshest, cruelest words. What have you done to me, Bernadette? Poured a potion in my drink? Tainted my food? How else do I come up with an answer for this? Of course all women have power over me. I've knelt before many — and made promises and pledges. But usually their spells last only a while, a night at most. Then I am on my way, glad to be rid of 'em. Only you, Darling, I keep coming back to. Sometimes, I think, against my will. I don't even believe it's love I feel for you. But something stronger.

We married, Tom and I, in a civil ceremony performed fast and plainly before a justice of the peace. In time I carried a child. This was to my astonishment. "Why, Doll-baby?" spoke Tom. "Women have babies every day of the week." Typical women, yes, was my answer. Perhaps I was one after all.

And in readying for the birth I sewed a miniature gown, a masterwork of satin and silver thread. While I worked I craved the wateriness of bell pepper, the brine of lemons, the aftertaste of cucumber. Happiness was now my fate, I thought.

But here was the thing, it was not meant to last. The child, a daughter, died. Tom died. Only I recovered from the fever. I woke, first in a dream, but then waking for real to a white hospital room.

Now I will get to the point. Quickly, because time grows short. Because it is painful to declare one's true self. Quick, I will get to the point.

Upon waking I cried. Not out of grief or misery, not yet. But out of gladness. That I was alive. This is my confession, however unbearable; it was thrilling to be the chosen one to live.

9) "You'll get your comeuppance," the old man said. I had not seen him ever before or since. On a corner of Piedmont Street he stood near me.

"What you say to me, Mister?" I asked, tilting my head. Between us, a staring contest that I won; his heavy-browed eyes darting away. But he had more to say.

"You'll get comeuppance, for sure. Though I won't live to see the day."

The light changed, and I crossed. What direction he took, I don't know.

10) One can become arrogant, surviving so much; surviving everyone, surviving one's own child, surviving the loss of love. And still the desire to go on; strong as ever. (There were two trees; one they reached but not the other. And on that second tree grows tantalizing fruit, deliciously scented. Whose mouth would not water for it?)

A day came when I faced a woman whose prime had passed. Black shiny crescents curved beneath her eyes, her jowls had slackened. She had a fleshy nose, and white flowed in her hair.

Bravely yet casually as a street whore, she unbuttoned her dress, and I saw her breasts were mere reminiscences (although mine, during my marriage to Tom, when I was at my happiest, had been full and plump with wine and cream and salt).

It was a different woman I became acquainted with that day. I studied her until I knew her. Then I smiled at her with acceptance because she and I would be companions for a long time to come.

I witnessed the deterioration of Piedmont Street also. First the bread factory closed and then many of the smaller businesses, windows crashed by a stone's throw or the flight of starlings, their flimsy doors barricaded. A pawnshop stood in place of the bank, and it drew as its customers thieves and addicts and the luckless.

I still swept the steps of my dressmaker's shop although the street itself was perpetually littered and my small effort could make no difference. With a curse I didn't mean, I chased away the poor mangy stray from the shade of the awning. "Get," I shouted, hitting its tattered rump with the broom. "Go find yourself someplace else to die, you miserable creature." It was such a day! Indian summer's vast, starry glare of unshifting heat.

This was when the street preacher started to appear. For the fourth day in a row he stood in front of the now ruined theater and for hours on end he preached there, ranting about hell and fire and sin. Oh, what a red, red sore he was! What a nuisance.

"I should call the police and have him arrested."

"For what?" asked my helper. Her name was Claire and though she was good-natured she was next to useless. Right now she was ripping out a simple stitch for the fourth time. Also every sleeve she tried to sew was bound to be puckered, her buttonholes confusions of loops and knots. Her efforts at zippers, pfffft! Doomed crooked-spined monstrosities!

For a moment more I wincingly watched her

damage the seam. Then I rubbed my exhausted eyes (so frequently I had to rest them now, it seemed; a worry I kept strictly to myself, for months it had been this way), and continued with nearly the same fury. "He's a disturbance to the peace! He's crazy or drunk. And what few customers I now have left he'll do me the favor of driving away."

"That's Daniel," she said, finally undoing the wayward stitching. She lifted her face to check the clock, which showed an hour and a half to go before quitting, so she had plenty of opportunity, I figured, to commit the same error at least four more times.

"I think Daniel should let alone the rum."

"But he's not a drinking man, not anymore. What he says is that he's been called." She shrugged a bare tawny shoulder and pushed aside her bangs. "He's only trying to save us."

Resuming my own task at hand, I tried to finish fixing a crest to a blazer despite the blurriness in my eyes. A red-apple pincushion sat on the table in front of me. But I barely saw it, its lopsided shape, its brashness of color.

Sighing, I put aside the blazer with the half-attached crest. I knew even then I would never finish it.

While in the background the lunatic spoke further, continuing his portrait of flames. And when finally he stopped it was wide-eyed Claire, still holding the mangled cloth, who spoke, posing the question she apparently had been waiting to ask.

"Is it true," she began in the hush, "that if you want something very much you should slit the throat of a rooster and rob a grave?"

"Oh, Child," I said with more tolerance and warmth than I felt toward her. "Those things were long ago and before my time. And who knows if such methods really worked anyway.

"Besides," I went further, and yes, I was meaning to tease her. "What is it you want so dearly?"

"Many things," she answered with such seriousness.

❖

I passed a church. But instead of thinking I should kneel before its massive oak doors and beg for my soul, as many thought I should, I considered it as a construction of wood and cement and glass that would stand a hundred years, two hundred years, perhaps a thousand, living longer than its builders (men, I have watched them, humble and without distinction, flawed in ordinariness; some comical-looking and vulgar, others mean and obnoxious in their ways, yet their soiled hands capable of building cathedrals and museums, schools and hospitals), who probably rest in Piedmont Street Cemetery, and so was not each and every singular brick, though laid in the most stupid, mindless, dullness of workman's toil, in its own way but a poor approach toward immortality?

❖

February, and with it rains had begun, torrential and punishing. The first drenching unleashed a pounding on the pavement, then eased into a more even temperament that hit the tin spots on the roof musically. After that, more rain came in an unusually furious season. A rain could last three days and nights without cease, or it could halt for small periods of relief, during which stood puddles with the still, placid surfaces of stepping-stones. But it was the steady drizzles that made me familiar with madness — if I reached my arm my fingertips could almost graze the rim: of its sleeplessness, of its tears, of its grim truth that this cry of "No More" is the final one and must be heeded.

How I missed the labor and loveliness of hanging clothes on the line to dry, and I wanted to hear again the nightly racket of crickets.

Throughout it all Daniel preached. That self-proclaimed archangel! That shabby herald! He shouted about curses and the rains fell peculiarly. I suppose like an omen.

(And I began to curse Daniel. Just as he cursed us, I cursed him. And I cursed the dusk that was steadfast and pitiless in its fall upon me.)

At the end of February the rains stopped and I was blind. So I closed and shuttered the shop. And I went home.

11) Because I did not care for the company I kept, I stayed to myself, within the shelter of my house bought so many years ago.

A housekeeper was hired to do my shopping and errands. During our first meeting I felt her broad features but nothing was revealed to me. Luckily it turned out that she was kindly. She could be trusted. The porcelain shepherd boy, the ivory horse, they could have brought something at the Piedmont Street pawnshop. Yet each stayed (as my searching fingers made certain) in its proper place on the mantel, put exactly back in its place until the next time she picked it up to mop the surface with her dust rag. In short time I came to know her rubber-soled footfall on the porch planks; still I'd wait until she called, "Yoo hoo, Miz Bernadette," before I unchained the door.

A day came when the steps were not hers, the measurements of pacing and weight differed; there was a squeak in the shoes. I waited, my heart frightened; finally, the stranger went away.

Soon enough, I heard my housekeeper's plain, familiar approach.

"You want some coffee, Miz Bernadette?" she asked, once the laundry was done.

"Yes, your coffee is good. Strong like coffee should be."

What did she tell the others of me (for they had not forgotten me), the strange old woman drinking her coffee alone in a parlor meant for visitors but to which no visitors are welcome? Does she herself forget that at first she used to sing? Until she too became silent.

Except for inquiring, "Can I go now, Miz Bernadette? The kitchen's all clean."

"Of course, you may go. I'll be fine."

And I would continue to sit in my chair, in the dimness. Yes, there I sat and sat. How many years passed in this way? Yet I cling to this very life, standstill in a constant midnight. My own breaths in and out; that was the tick-tock of time. While all along they felt my presence. No, they had not forgotten me. (All too well I stayed in their minds.) They had not ceased hating. But they were patient.

Then through the open window I heard my

housekeeper arguing. She was not the one I just mentioned. Oh, no, there have been so many housekeepers since her, and not all so honest by the way — the shepherd boy, the candlesticks and hurricane lamp, a picture from the wall went missing. So this was the latest in a long list (of Mimis and Karens and Yvonnes and Josephinas), her voice was young and it was raised, feistily insulting her opponent's intelligence and that of the mother who chose to bear him; as well she mockingly pitied the shame he must feel at the witlessness of any children unfortunate enough to be born of his seed, if indeed there was truly a woman so lacking in dignity and good sense she would lower herself to copulate with him.

She came inside, hotly explaining, "That was the man hired to take care of the yard. He said he won't do it no more. Let the dandelions grow a foot high and ivy where it wants, he says too bad. He says it don't bother him none; let the vines choke the damned house! he had the nerve to declare. Let the bushes cover the windows and keep out the warmth of the sun! And he says nobody else gonna do it either.

"Miz Bernadette, people can be superstitious even in this day and age. People can be ignorant when they choose.

"But what I think is everybody's just gone plain crazy around here!"

She went to do her chores. In the meantime, I sat alone and understood that this was the first sign. That patient they would no longer be.

12) I must hurry to finish up my story.

The second sign was the street preacher coming to me in a dream. Daniel, tall as a tower, dressed in a threadbare suit. How fierce his eyes were. He held in one hand his black Bible and in the other a bouquet of bird of paradise, like a bright, bright torch.

Came the third sign. A tree grew through the floorboards of the parlor. Sharply my sightless eyes witnessed this; I saw the trunk and the full, fresh leaves, and in the room was the musty scent of a strange fruit. I was not dreaming. It was day and I heard my young housekeeper moving about, doing her work.

The tree did not disappear when she came into

the room, saying, "All done, Miz Bernadette. So can I get going now? My baby girl is waiting on me."

I did not speak right away. Eventually, I said, "Yes, you may go."

Behind her the door shuts.

And now they send their children to gather in my front yard. (Sweet innocent babes, ha! They are to be feared!) Listen to the song they sing. Their tender voices sing:

Witch. Witch. Wicked Woman.
What is your name?
(Bernadette.)
Have you no shame? (Bernadette.)
(For your evil scheme.)
We know your name!
Bernadette!

A woman with mighty lungs screams why should her sister die and I live? Another accuses me of being a thousand years old and of, as I have heard so often before, bringing vengeance upon them.

The rock shatters my window.

When I flinch, it is merely because tiny shards of glass prick my cheeks. At once, intruders flow in. Plodding and crashing. I hear their noise. As if an echo. For something in me has been long prepared for this day.

So the time is here.

(Yet I will not pray, not to their God. Nor do I call to their devil.) Already their nearness circles me.

One of them, close enough that I feel his breath, says with odd respect, with dear assurance, "The street burns, Miz Bernadette. Now you will burn too. Don't worry too much. I think it will be over quick."

Yes, quick, quick, I think. It is always over too quick.

There is the stench of hair burning.

And I remember what good Creole mothers tell their daughters. Never let a strand of your hair fall into the hands of enemies. Gather all them up, from your brush, your collar, the porcelain sink. Wrap the strands in tissue paper and burn the tiny bundle in a shallow dish. Never allow your enemies to get hold of your hairs. For harm they mean to do to you. But if you want power over your foes, then pluck their hair out.

I laugh, they cannot understand why.

Their fear of me is potent, it will not fade. Their judgment is eternal. Their lies and accusations will be retold; each new generation will hear stories of me.

When an herb garden is raided. When they sense a pair of eyes peering into a window. They will query, "Bernadette?" When a baby wakes from a peaceable sleep, and howls, they will whisper, "Bernadette."

Although what little comfort that is to me now.

❖

What a crowd in the street! People moving in chaotic parade, with shouts and shrieks. Instead of newborns, arms cradle plucked chickens. Bulged fists choke the necks of rum bottles. Backs haul maplewood china cabinets to the destinations of their new homes.

❖

After
It Burned to the Ground

The woman came out, a bright red kerchief covering her hair, ends tied at her nape. She swept her porch clean of smoke-colored ashes that still were drifting from the sky in the only blizzard this street would ever see.

Elliot Piciotto

The Author

Yolanda Barnes lives in Los Angeles, where she was born—a city some have called Paradise. Her window has included a view of blooming jacaranda trees, warring hummingbirds, and the flames of the riots. She graduated Phi Beta Kappa from the University of Southern California, where she majored in Journalism, and received her MFA from the University of Virginia. Her short fiction has appeared in *TriQuarterly, Ploughshares,* and the *O. Henry* and *Pushcart Prize* collections.

Acknowledgements to *Ploughshares* and *TriQuarterly* literary magazines and The Pushcart Prize and O. Henry Prize collections. And much gratitude to Kristina McGrath, who poured her heart and soul into editing this work.